to the world

JY,
to the world

BY KAI SHAPPLEY AND LISA BUNKER

Clarion Books
An Imprint of HarperCollins*Publishers*

The authors and the publisher have made a one-time donation to the ACLU.

Clarion Books is an imprint of HarperCollins Publishers.

Joy, to the World
Text copyright © 2023 by Kai Shappley and Lisa Bunker
Illustrations copyright © 2023 by Noah Grigni
All rights reserved. Printed in the United States of America. No part of this book may be used or reproduced in any manner whatsoever without written permission except in the case of brief quotations embodied in critical articles and reviews. For information address HarperCollins Children's Books, a division of HarperCollins Publishers, 195 Broadway, New York, NY 10007.
www.harpercollinschildrens.com

Library of Congress Cataloging-in-Publication Data
Names: Shappley, Kai, author. | Bunker, Lisa, author.
Title: Joy, to the world / by Kai Shappley and Lisa Bunker.
Description: First edition. | New York : Clarion Books, [2023] | Audience: Ages 8–12. | Audience: Grades 4–6. | Summary: Joy, a twelve-year-old transgender girl, fights for her right to cheer in Texas.
Identifiers: LCCN 2022036213 | ISBN 9780063242753 (hardcover)
Subjects: CYAC: Transgender people—Fiction. | Cheerleading—Fiction. | Texas—Fiction.
Classification: LCC PZ7.1.S48345 Jo 2023 | DDC [Fic]—dc23
LC record available at https://lccn.loc.gov/2022036213

Typography by Sarah Nichole Kaufman
23 24 25 26 27 LBC 5 4 3 2 1

First Edition

My very first book is dedicated to every politician—from local school boards, to state legislatures, to the halls of DC—who have attacked trans kids, our families, our doctors, and our allies. You've made us politically knowledgeable, motivated, and fierce. It's exciting to know our generation will be in charge soon.

—K.S.

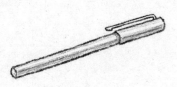

This one is for all the parents, teachers, and other adults who affirm and support the trans kids in their care. Thank you! You are saving lives. —L.B.

one

IT WAS JUST supposed to be an afternoon of pool fun to beat the Texas heat. Joy was not expecting to fall in love.

It was the first full week of summer vacation after sixth grade, and Joy's good friend, Maxine Newman—Max for short—had invited her over to cool off. The hot, humid air lay over everything like a wet wool blanket. It felt hard to breathe.

"Come on through to the back," Max said when she opened the big front door of her family's elegant two-story suburban house. "Did you bring your bathing suit?"

"Actually, if you don't mind, I'd rather just sit in the shade."

"Really? You don't want to swim? That's cool."

The pool was encircled by pretty landscaping with a concrete fountain, a fancy swing set, a couple of big shade trees, and a table with an umbrella. On the way through the kitchen, they picked up lemonade and crunchy snacks.

Someone who saw the two girls together might have thought they were sisters. They both had the same brown hair, a sprinkle of freckles across their cheeks, and skin that tanned easily in the Texas sun. Joy's hair was longer, reaching down to the middle of her back in a long, straight fall. Max's was cut shoulder-length and had a touch of curl to it.

In the pool, Max's older sister, Priscilla, and her three friends were trying to do something, but Joy couldn't figure out what. They were in the part of the pool where the water came up to just under their arms, standing all clustered together, and Priscilla and two of the friends kept throwing the fourth girl up into the air, high enough to try to do a sort of flying dance move. Then when she came down again, it looked like they were trying to catch her, but mostly they were diving out of the way. Each time they all laughed about it and tried again.

"What are they doing?" Joy asked.

"They're trying to do a pike open."

"What's a pike open?"

Max dropped her mouth open in an exaggerated expression of surprise. "You don't know what a pike open is?"

"No. What is it?"

"It's a basket toss in cheer. You know what cheer is, right?"

"Not really, no."

This time Max's surprise was real. "How can you live in Appleton and not know cheer? It's like the official sport of Texas. Well, besides football, of course."

Joy felt a little defensive now, but Max wasn't being mean—Max was never mean—so she felt comfortable saying, "You know we only moved here four months ago."

"Oh, right. Remind me again, where did y'all live before?"

"Minnesota."

"Gucci." Max pushed her hair to the side of her forehead. "Anyway, we have got to get you up to speed right away, because you can't live in Texas and not know cheer."

From the water came the sound of a shriek and a splash, followed by laughter. The two girls looked back toward the pool. Max said, "Okay, check it out. See Priscilla and her friend Renee, there, standing on the sides? They're the bases. And then Claire, the girl with the green bathing suit, she's the spotter. She stands behind. Allie is the flyer. She's the one they throw up in the air and catch." As they watched, the girls in the pool clustered together again, did a countdown, and shouted like they were pushing extra hard. Allie flew higher than before and did the dance move, touching her toes and then arching her back. When she came down, the three other girls stayed in close and caught her. Then all four of them whooped and danced in the water.

"Yes!" Max hollered. "That was totally dope! They did it!"

Joy's heart was beating in her ears, and she felt a warm rush go through her body that had nothing to do with the swampy summer air. Something about what Priscilla and her friends were doing called powerfully to her. "Max, can you show me more?"

"Sure. We need more lemonade anyway. Let's go inside and check out some videos."

Inside the house, the AC felt cold after the heat of the backyard. Between that and the excitement she was feeling, Joy began to shiver. Max's dad was sitting on the couch, scrolling on his phone. "Hello, girls," he said. "All done swimming today?"

"Joy wants to learn about cheer," Max said. "Can we use the computer in your office?"

"You sure can, kiddo. Go right ahead."

In the office Joy and Max pushed aside the rolling office chair and stood side by side at the big desk. Max did a quick search, and then they were watching videos together of people dressed in flashy spandex and sequins, dancing and vaulting and spinning and flying through the air.

Joy gripped the edge of the desk. Her body buzzed with excitement. All her life she had been an athletic kid, loving the feeling of throwing herself through space. She had learned to do a cartwheel when she was four. The acrobatics in cheer looked like the most fun thing to do in the world. Plus, the clothes and sparkles and the big bows in the girls' hair looked incredibly fabulous. Joy felt her heart open like a flower . . . and that was the moment she fell in love with cheer.

* * *

Most nights before turning out her light, Joy wrote in a journal. The night of the day she fell in love with cheer, she lay looking around her room for a minute before starting her entry. The room was small, with a low ceiling. The one little window looked out at the back side of the hedge in their tiny front yard, and several times a minute the sound of cars passing on their busy road could be heard. With her mom's help, Joy had done what she could to make the room prettier and more pleasant. Joy especially liked the colorful cloth thumbtacked to the ceiling, and the strings of soft white lights strung around the walls.

Joy had started her first journal when she was eight, and she had carefully written *Joy's Journal* on the first page. Then she noticed that both words started with "Jo," which was the reason for how, four years later, she started her entry each night. She rolled over onto her stomach and started to write.

Hey Jojo,

Today I learned what I want to do for the rest of my life! Well, besides drawing and sewing, my other two loves. Cheer is my destiny. I want to be a flyer. It's a good thing I'm so small for my age.

After Max and I watched videos, we went out and practiced handstands and stuff on the lawn until it got too hot. I couldn't wait to tell Mom, even though I wasn't sure what she would say. I wish she liked girly stuff as much as I do, just like I wish she cared as much about church as I do. Anyway, she said, "That's nice," in that distracted way she does sometimes, so that was pretty okay, I guess.

Of course, Will had to comment. He said cheer was stupid, because why should girls be on the side, cheering for the boys? He said it was sexist. I tried to tell him it wasn't like that, that it is its own sport, but he never listens, and then Mom did that sigh she does and rubbed between her eyes. My brother is so basic.

After dinner, I watched more videos and found a list of cheer words to learn, and tomorrow I'm going over to Max's house again to learn some more. This is so totally lit! I hope I can sleep.

God bless Mom, and Max, and her sister and her sister's friends, and cheer, and, fine, God bless Will too, even though he is such a jerk all the time.

two

JOY STARTED WATCHING every cheer movie and show and video and visiting every cheer website she could find. She and Max and another friend of Max's named Steph Carter formed the Sparkle Squad, which was the name they came up with together for their team of three. The squad had one mission: to all make it onto the Appleton East Middle School cheer team when seventh grade started in the fall. Tryouts were the last week of summer before school, and it was reportedly a very hard team to make, especially because everyone had to try out again every year.

When it came to tryouts, Joy faced a challenge the other two girls didn't. She had to get her mother to agree. Jenny Simmons tended to worry, too much in Joy's opinion, and to be cautious about things that might cost money. Joy found it difficult to stay silent when she was feeling so eager, but she knew from experience that it was best to wait for the right moment. A morning came when Mom was humming as she made her coffee. "Mom?" Joy said.

"Yes, sweetheart?"

"You know I'm having so much fun with Max and Steph, learning cheer."

"Yes, I know."

"It's really good for me, physically and mentally." These were ideas Joy knew her mother liked.

"I'm glad to hear it."

"So, what I was wondering was, can I try out for cheer at school in the fall?" Mom stopped humming and frowned. "Please? I just love it so much."

"I'll think about it," Mom said, but she smiled and nodded as she said it, and Joy knew she was in.

At first when Max suggested inviting Steph to join the Sparkle Squad, Joy wasn't sure it was a good idea. The upside was that, of the three of them, Steph was the only one who was already on the cheer team. She had a lot of skills, and there was so much that Joy could learn from her. The downside was that Steph was an intense, bossy girl, not afraid to tell you that you were doing something wrong in a way that sometimes seemed just plain mean. Steph had pale skin but black hair and eyebrows, and when she frowned, Joy felt intimidated.

Joy never said anything, though, because in her research she was learning that in cheer, attitude and teamwork were just as important as strength and flexibility and skill. Cheerleaders were not just athletes—they were team players and ambassadors of school spirit.

Learning this only made Joy love cheer more. It was like there were two teams, the cheer team itself, and then the bigger team of the whole school, in which the cheer team had an important role. It felt just right. It felt like home.

Another reason Joy never said anything when Steph was bossy or mean was that Steph's house, even though it was almost as small and old as Joy's, had a trampoline in the backyard, which was excellent for practicing jumps. Mostly they practiced at Max's house, because it had by far the best shade, and because of Priscilla, who was in high school cheer and who would come outside sometimes and coach them.

They only practiced at Joy's house once, and it didn't go well, because the Simmons' tiny backyard had no shade, no trampoline, and hardly any lawn. Besides that, there was a lot of noise from the auto body shop on the other side of the high wooden fence in back; and Viking, the Simmons' rambunctious black lab, went nuts watching them and got in the way if he was outside, or barked and barked through the sliding glass door if they shut him inside.

By the end of the first week with the Sparkle Squad, Joy had made a vow to turn herself into the best possible cheerleader she could be. There was a lot to learn—jumps and tumbling and stunts. There was also the challenge of getting her body in shape. In particular, at the start of the summer, she was not as flexible as she needed to be. To be in cheer, you needed to be able to kick your legs high and bend them every which way, and at first Joy's body just wouldn't do what she wanted it to.

She loved a challenge, though, so she set herself a specific goal: by the end of the summer, she wanted to do a scorpion. In the video she watched over and over, a girl who looked like a ballet dancer kicked one leg up and back, so high that her foot was behind her head. Then she reached both arms back over her shoulders and caught the raised foot in both hands, so that her arms and legs and curved back made a circle.

In June, practicing in her room, Joy wasn't even close to being able to catch her foot behind her head, so she worked first on doing a good arabesque, which was standing on one leg and pointing the other leg straight out behind your body, then leaning forward, with your upper body arching up and your arms held out to the sides. That was easy, so then she moved on to a scale, which was holding one leg straight up and to the side and lifting it with one hand, while putting the other arm up to form a V position. She could do a pretty good scale by the end of July, but she still couldn't catch her foot behind her head. Luckily, her body seemed like it was willing to get more flexible, so she just kept stretching and working, and finally, in the second week of August, she caught her foot!

She knew it wasn't a very good scorpion yet, but it was still a thrill. She was alone when she did it, practicing in the weedy backyard, despite the machine shop noise and the sticky late summer heat. Max was on vacation with her family, and Joy didn't want to practice with with Steph alone, who was still more Max's friend than hers. She had to tell somebody, though, so she ran inside, looking for her mother.

The poky kitchen with its old banged-up cabinets and brown-green linoleum floor was empty. So was the tiny laundry room. In her bedroom, maybe? Joy ran down the one short hall. The door was open a little bit, and she barged through. Her mom was sitting on her bed with her head bowed, and she had a tissue in her hand. Joy screeched to a halt. "I'm sorry," she said.

Mom looked up. She had tear tracks on her face. "It's okay, honey."

Joy knew that her mother got sad and stressed sometimes. Joy's father had left when Joy was still a baby, so Mom was on her own raising Joy and Will. Joy moved the rest of the way around the bed and gave her mom a hug. Her mother hugged her back and cried a little more. They didn't need to say anything. Then Mom wiped her eyes and patted herself on the knees. "Back to it," she said. "What did you want to tell me?"

Joy shared her scorpion news, and her mom said encouraging things. She had always been the kind of mom who supported what her kids wanted to do once she decided it was okay, even if she didn't care about those things herself, and even though she also worried. A couple of times she had warned Joy not to stretch quite so much quite so fast, and Joy actually paid attention to that after a time when she tried harder than usual to do a split and felt a ripping sensation on the inside of her leg, and had to stop practicing for a couple of days.

There was another thing to worry about too. They had quickly learned that cheer was expensive, and the Simmons family did not have any money to spare. So Mom fretted. But she also always remembered to say, "If it's important to you, sweetheart, we'll find a way," and Joy loved her for it.

Hey Jojo,

I finally did a scorpion today! It wasn't very good yet, but it was still amazing to do it. I can't wait to show Max and Steph.

I wish I knew how to help Mom feel less sad. I think it would help if she listened more to Reverend Morales when she talks about hope and trusting in the Lord, but that one time I said something to her about that, it was like she didn't hear me. Maybe I could put together a cheer routine just for her, but I guess that probably wouldn't help. She still doesn't really get how much I love cheer, but at least she's letting me do it.

Ten days until tryouts! And only six practice days, after Max gets back from vacation. I hope I make the team! It's all I ever wanted in the whole world.

God bless Mom and Will, and Max and Steph, and God bless cheer!

three

ONCE MAX GOT home from vacation, the Sparkle Squad put all their energy in their last week of practice into learning skills they would have to demonstrate at tryouts. There were some basic drills to do, which Joy felt confident about, and a routine to learn, which made her more nervous. She could do all the moves—that wasn't the problem. The hardest things were a toe touch and a herkie, and she was good at both. The problem was that sometimes in the middle of the routine she couldn't quite remember fast enough what the next move was, so she hesitated, or even, once or twice, had to bail out. When that happened, she didn't need Steph's sarcastic eyebrows to know that it wasn't good enough.

At one August practice in the Newmans' big playroom—they were practicing inside because of the thunderstorm happening outside, making a field of splashes out of the swimming pool—Max's big sister, Priscilla, had helpful advice. "Lots of cheerleaders have a hard time remembering routines," she said. "The answer is practice, practice, and more practice."

So Joy practiced every day. She practiced with the Sparkle Squad, and at home on her own. Remembering her mom's warnings about overdoing it, she sometimes only hinted at the moves with gentle gestures, but in her mind she was cementing the order in place, until, by the last few days before tryouts, the routine was running on a loop in her head, all day and all night long.

When tryout day finally came and her mom drove her to the school, Joy was feeling a mix of confident, nervous, and excited. She was wearing her favorite lucky shorts, the lavender ones her grandmother back in Minnesota had helped her sew, and an Appleton East Cheer T-shirt that Priscilla had given her. At the dollar store Mom had helped her pick out a purple bow with sequins for her hair.

The Sparkle Squad had decided they would all meet in the parking lot before tryouts. When they got together, Max looked as excited as Joy felt. Steph never showed her feelings much, but she had on her intensity face, tight around the eyes and mouth.

Toward the end of the summer, the Sparkle Squad had started making up cheers of their own. Now, they did one of the short ones for getting pumped up, standing in a tight triangle with their hands together in the middle, and chanting:

Sparkle Squad is on the floor.
Look out, world, here we come!
Joy the rock star,
Max the GOAT,
Steph the queen,
Here we come!
Goooooooo, Sparkle Squad!

Then they went in together, ready to dazzle the judges.

Inside, a scary surprise was waiting. At least,

it was scary for Joy. She had assumed that they would get to try out together, but it turned out not to be so. They were given paper numbers to pin to their shirts, and then they were called into the gym in groups of three by number, and you didn't get to pick who the other two were.

Joy's heart started to race. "Wait, what?" she said. "I don't know if I can do this without you guys."

"It's always like this," Steph said, in her usual hard voice. She shook her head.

Max was kinder, as always. "Come on, Joy, you've got this. You know the routine as well as either of us, and if you're going to be on the team, you're going to have to be able to cheer next to anyone. Just remember to give it everything you've got."

Joy smiled at her friend, but she was still scared, and before she had figured out a way to get her confidence back, her number was called. She gave Max one last frightened glance and then went through the door into the gym.

The judges were the cheer coach, Emily Porter, and four mom-aged ladies. Coach Porter was in her twenties and looked younger, almost like a teenager. She was a small but muscular woman, a former flyer, with dark brown skin and tight curly hair cut short. She stood a little apart, watching with a still, unreadable face. The four other judges sat on folding chairs at a table with clipboards and papers in front of them, and they looked like they might be former cheerleaders. You could see it in their pulled-back ponytails and heavy eyebrow makeup, and in their faces, which had different versions of the same kind of intensity that was often visible on Steph's face.

Joy's fear spiked as she walked up to the line, but as she took her position, she felt something shift inside her. She wasn't going to let Steph or these judges or anyone make her feel like she wasn't good enough. Was she or was she not in love with cheer? She was. Had she or had she not practiced and studied and trained for hours and hours all summer long? She had. And didn't she have just as much intensity inside her as anyone else on the whole planet? Why, yes, she did. As she put her hands on her hips for the first drill, she tossed her ponytail back, held up her chin, and stared at the four women behind the table. "I can so do this," she whispered to herself.

Hey Jojo,

Tryouts went pretty well, I think. I messed up one part—the toe touch—but I kept moving, so it was seamless. Fingers crossed! Max said hers didn't go well, but she's always hard on herself, so I bet she did better than she thinks. Steph didn't say much, so I don't know how she did, but probably fine. She was already on the team last year, and she's just really good at cheer.

Now comes the waiting part. I hate waiting! They said we'll get a phone call either way the Saturday before schools starts. That's five days that I have to wait. This is going to be the longest week of my life.

If I don't make the team, I will be so bummed. But Mom and Priscilla both said the same thing about that. They said if you don't get in, you can practice some more and try again next year. It's just like when I missed the toe touch. I found my place and kept going. So either way I won't give up. I am still praying that I get in, though, praying so hard.

God bless Mom and Will, and Max and Priscilla and Steph and Coach Porter and those nice judge ladies, and God bless cheer!

Max + Steph + me

four

AS THEY GOT closer to the day the call was supposed to come, Joy had an idea. She figured she wasn't going to be able to sleep the night before, so why not have a sleepover? It would be fun to get the Sparkle Squad together for something besides a practice. She waited until her mom was humming as she made coffee again, and asked.

"Sure, sweetheart," Mom said. "I'm glad you're making friends. You could ask them to come early enough for dinner, too, if you like."

"Thanks, Mom," Joy said, and she really was grateful, even if she couldn't help also wishing that her mom would show that much enthusiasm for cheer. Still, it was good that Joy was going to be able to entertain her friends. It felt like making things even, since all but one of the Sparkle Squad practices had happened at the other two girls' houses.

Joy felt a little nervous about asking Steph, because even after training together all summer long, she wasn't sure that the other girl liked her, but she made herself do it anyway. "Hey, you guys," she said, as they took turns on the trampoline in Steph's backyard. "Do you want to come over for a sleepover on Friday?"

"If my parents say it's okay!" said Max.

Joy watched Steph anxiously. Steph's eyes shifted back and forth like she was thinking, but then she smiled, which she hardly ever did. "I have to ask my mom," she said. "But, yeah, thank you for the invitation." Joy wondered if underneath her tough shell Steph was shy, or afraid to show something softer. To the growing list of goals in her head she added, *Make real friends with Steph.*

Joy had fun picking what dinner would be—she settled on a grilled hot dog feast with all the fixings—and planning the fun for the evening, which was watching a new cheer movie that had just come out. Max and Steph were bringing sleeping bags and pads for their places on the floor in Joy's room, and Joy thought about that and decided she didn't want to be up on the bed if her friends were on the floor, so she got out her bag and pad too.

Her nerves came back for a while as she sat on the couch in the living room, watching for parent-chauffeurs to pull up to the curb, but when her two friends arrived, one right after the other, the party started on a good note and just kept going. Within minutes they were shrieking and laughing as they did what tumbling they could in the tiny yard, with Viking romping around them, and soon after that they were munching on tasty crisp-skinned hot dogs and watching their movie.

There was an interesting moment when Will came through, going to his room to play video games with headphones on so he wouldn't have to hear them. He looked at the screen for a second and said sarcastically, "Look at the pretty little pompom girls."

Joy blushed and searched her mind for a reply, but to her surprise it was Max who answered. She gave Will a look like he was an annoying insect and said, "You say that like it's a bad thing."

Steph gave Joy's big brother a withering look to match Max's and added, "The word you are looking for is 'athletes.' Cheer is the best of dance and tumbling and circus, all mashed up together in one amazing sport."

"Oh, well, sorry then," Will said, trying for more sarcasm, but Joy could tell it was forced. He had not been expecting anyone to answer back. He was beaten and he knew it. He turned and retreated down the hall.

Joy was delighted. "Wow, you guys, that was lit," she said, and all three girls shared a smile. Steph held up a hand, Joy high-fived her, and as they went back to watching the movie, Joy savored the warm glow she felt inside. That had felt like a big step in the making-friends-with-Steph project.

Later, when they were lying on the floor together in sleeping bags, they talked a little about their lives. Joy told about her dad leaving the family and about having to move so her mom could find work, which Steph had not known before. Steph, it turned out, no longer had a dad in her life either. Joy could sense from how Steph told the story that there was some trouble around that, but she didn't feel comfortable asking for more details. It seemed clear, though, that even though Steph was only about to start seventh grade, she had already had some trouble in her life.

Before they finally turned out the light, the three girls made a pact: no matter who made the cheer team, whether it was none or one or two or all three of them, they would keep the Sparkle Squad going too. They would stay a team, no matter what. Joy smiled as she drifted off toward sleep, just as dawn was beginning to lighten the window behind its pulled-down shade.

With her friends sleeping on either side of her, there was no way to write in her journal, but she knew what she would write if she could. *Hey Jojo, I still want to get on the team so bad, but if I don't, I'm going to try to remember this moment right now, because I'm already on a team, and it feels so good to be on a team with friends. God bless Mom and Will, and God bless the Sparkle Squad.*

five

ON SATURDAY AFTERNOON Joy's phone kept going off, and it kept not being the call. First it was Steph, texting to say she'd made the team. Steph was so excited she even put in a grinny face. Joy texted back to say congratulations. Then she put the phone down on the kitchen table and moved nervously around the cramped living room, chewing on her fingernails. Mom watched from the kitchen, where she was washing the dishes.

After ten minutes the phone came to life again, this time with Max's special ring. Joy pounced on it, and then spent five minutes saying, "Uh-huh, uh-huh" while her best friend gushed about getting on the team as well. Max ended by saying she was sure that Joy would make the team too, but

Joy was beginning to get a stomachache. She was sure she had been passed over.

She put the phone back on the table, fidgeted around for a few minutes more, and then said to her mom, "I can't do this anymore. I'll be in my room under the covers."

Fifteen minutes later, her mom tugged gently on her heel. Joy threw off the covers and looked up with a flushed face and damp cheeks. Mom handed her the phone.

"Joy?" said a voice.

"Yes, this is Joy."

"This is Coach Porter. I'm calling to congratulate you. You're going to be cheering for Appleton East this year."

Joy's scream of happiness brought Viking barking and running, and then her mother held her while she cried happy tears.

Joy had no idea how much work cheer was going to be. When the schedule came, Mom suggested they go over it together, and they both had to take a couple of deep breaths. Almost every square on the calendar they were writing in had something in it. There were three practices a week, plus pep rallies and games—football to start, once a week, and later in the fall, basketball too, sometimes twice a week. Besides that, she was expected to fundraise and do community service. And there was also the part about how being on the cheer team was both an honor and a privilege, and how all team members were expected to follow a strict code of conduct, not just at school, but all the time.

It was a lot, and when Mom said in a careful voice, "You're going to be pretty busy, sweetheart," Joy gulped and nodded.

"I can do it, Mom," she said. "I have to. I'll do whatever it takes."

"I know you can. It's a good thing the school is close enough that you can walk if you have to, because I won't always be able to get off work to drive you. You know that when I'm the only librarian on duty, I have to stay. And Will won't have his license for a year yet."

Good, thought Joy. It would be no fun to have to get lots of rides from her obnoxious older brother. She didn't say anything out loud, though. She had a code of conduct to follow now.

Another expectation was that all members of the team had to have above a B-minus in all their classes, and as school started, Joy discovered right away that seventh grade was going to be harder than sixth, especially math. Her brain just did not like numbers—it never had—but up until now she had been able to scrape by. Her new assignments, getting ready for algebra next year, felt like a total mystery.

From the first day, Joy gave her challenging new schedule everything she had, and it went okay. It felt like she was always busy, and that was stressful sometimes, but mostly it felt good. At other times in her life she had struggled to get out of bed in the morning, but now there was no time for dozing and wandering in half dreams, avoiding the start of the day. There was too much to do. She started waking up before her alarm, folding the covers back, and getting up right away. She discovered that it could be pleasant to be the first person up, padding into the quiet kitchen to get breakfast started for everyone. Mom liked that part, and Joy enjoyed her praise.

Another bright spot was Joy's new coach. Officially, they were supposed to call her Coach Porter,

but girls who were doing well on the team, showing up every day and working hard, could get away
with calling her Coach Emily. Joy admired the
way Coach Emily held her body, like a dancer or
a gymnast, all the time, even when she was just
standing with a clipboard watching practice, and
she started trying to copy that unconscious grace.
She also loved her coach's attitude, which was the
perfect mix of toughness and kindness. From the
first practice on, Joy adored her new coach and
tried hard to please her.

The third week of practice, Joy thought of a way
to improve the big new routine they were working up for a football game in mid-October against
Basswood, Appleton East's biggest rival. It took
her a day to work up her nerve, but then during
a break in practice, she took the plunge. "Coach
Emily?"

"What's up, Joy?"

"Um . . . I . . ."

"Go ahead and speak your mind, Joy."

"I have an idea about the dance moves right at
the end."

"You do? Tell me."

Joy explained what she had in mind and then

held her breath. Coach Emily looked serious and didn't speak for a moment. Then she said, "Let's give it a try." She called the team back together and walked them through Joy's suggestion, asking Joy once or twice if they were doing it right. Some of the girls looked like they didn't like Joy's idea much, but Joy's eyes were on Coach Emily. "It's good," she said after they had tried it twice. "We'll keep it in." Joy spent the rest of the day glowing with pleasure. And it would be so exciting to do her own dance move at the big game.

One more thing about the new school year came as a pleasant surprise to Joy, and that was that, as a cheerleader, she was automatically at least somewhat popular. There were levels of popularity, and she couldn't compete with the girls who really wanted it and worked hard for it, but she didn't care about that. It was nice enough that there were other kids who knew who she was, and that mostly she was treated kindly by other students and by teachers and other grown-ups at the school. In sixth grade, she had felt like she was on the outside edge of things, looking in. Now she could tell that she was in the mix, and she liked that feeling a lot. Being in cheer helped her feel more like she belonged than she ever had before.

For four weeks, everything was perfect.

Then the phone call came.

six

THE PHONE CALL came just as Mom, Will, and Joy were all sitting down to breakfast together one Thursday morning in early October. Mom's phone did the warble she had programmed for unknown, outside numbers. She picked it up and looked at the screen. "Hmm," she said, "local number." She did a little shrug and tapped to answer. Joy and Will watched her listen. "Yes, it is," she said. Then she looked surprised and said, "Principal Davis. How can I help you this morning?" Joy and Will exchanged a look. Brent Davis was Joy's principal at Appleton East Middle School, and of course they both knew that it was not usually a good thing when your principal called. Joy searched her mind for a reason. Had she done something wrong without realizing? Had she broken the honor code?

For a minute Mom mostly listened, but her face told a story, going from curious to puzzled to angry. Joy felt an empty place open in her stomach. "Yes," Mom said, when she started talking again. "Yes, you know that she is. We had a meeting, remember?" More listening. Then, "Well, I don't see why it's suddenly an issue, after—" The voice Joy and Will could just hear, not loud enough to catch words, cut her off. Mom gave Joy a look that made the pit in her stomach sink deeper. Something was seriously wrong, and Joy was beginning to guess what it might be. Her face went hot, her breath caught, and she felt tears start to press behind her eyes.

"Well, needless to say, I think that's a horrible decision," Mom said. "Joy loves cheer. I've never seen her so dedicated to anything in her life." Joy felt the tears coming. "Yes, you can be certain that I will do that. Yes. No. No. I do have to say, I am deeply disappointed in you and in the school, both. Well, I'm sorry you feel that way, but I stand with my child and will respectfully speak my mind. Okay, yes, you too. Goodbye." Mom tapped to end the call.

For a moment the three members of the Simmons family looked silently at each other around the table. Joy was crying. She already knew. Mom's eyes were wet too, and even Will looked unusually sad and subdued. Mom got up, came around the table, and pulled Joy up into a hug. "Oh, sweetheart, I'm so sorry."

Through her tears, Joy said, "I'm off the team?" Mom made a sympathy face and nodded. "Because I'm trans?" Mom pressed her lips together and nodded again.

Joy felt like her heart was being ripped out of her body. She wailed, clutched her mother, and dissolved into sobs. When the first stormy minute had passed, she looked up with a tear-streaked face and said, "Can they do that? Can they really do that?"

"I'm not sure, sweetheart, but Principal Davis said there's a law that says that student athletes in Texas have to be on the team that aligns with their sex assigned at birth."

"That's not fair! And what about my dance move? I can't not be on the team when we play Basswood!"

"Of course it's not fair, sweetheart, but if there's a law, we have to follow it."

Unexpectedly, it was Will who spoke next. "What I'm wondering is, why now? If she can't be on the cheer team, why didn't they say so right from the beginning, instead of letting her in and then crushing her dreams?"

"I guess maybe no one connected the dots before. But now Principal Davis said that someone complained."

"Someone complained?" Joy said in a quivery voice. "But nobody knows."

"I guess someone must have found out."

"I've been outed?" Joy gasped. Up until now, only the principal, the school nurse, and a couple of teachers had known that Joy was transgender. She was living in stealth, as it was called, and it was meant to keep her safe.

"We don't know."

Will spoke up again. "Well, is there any way we can fight it?"

"I don't know that either," Mom answered. "But now that you bring it up, that's a good question." She turned back to Joy and held her face in both hands. "Joy, my darling girl, this is a blow, but it might not be the end of the story. There might be ways to fight."

"There might?"

"Yes, there might. First, we need more information. As Will points out, why now? And who complained? And who else knows?"

"How do we find all that out?"

"I'm going to take you to school right now and ask to talk to Principal Davis." Joy winced, and Mom said gently, "What is it, honey?"

"Do I . . . do I have to go to school today?" Joy's mouth twisted and a fresh tear tracked down one cheek. Being at school today seemed impossible. What would she say to Max and Steph when it came time to go to practice? And how could she face a whole school full of people without knowing who had learned her carefully kept secret and who had not?

Mom studied her daughter's face. "Hmm," she said. "I understand why you wouldn't want to. But, on the other hand, it's important to face your problems."

Will spoke again. "Today, though. Today we don't even know what the problem is."

Mom looked thoughtful. "That's true."

"Please?" Joy begged. "Please? Just one day? Until we know what's really going on?"

The two children watched their mother think. At last she nodded and said, "All right, you can stay home one day. You've had a nasty shock, and it's true you'd be entering a landscape full of unknowns."

"Thank you," Joy said fervently.

"You're welcome, sweetheart. I'll tell them you're not feeling well today when I go into the office. And I'll come home for lunch to check on you and tell you what I've learned."

seven

WHEN MOM AND WILL LEFT, Joy flopped on her bed and cried until she felt like she had no tears left. Then, exhausted, she dozed for a while. When she woke up, she stared at the ceiling. Then she sat in bed for a while and tried to work on her latest embroidery project, then did a little sketching, but she couldn't focus, so she got up, trailed into the living room, and turned on the TV. It was too painful to watch any of her new favorite cheer shows or movies, so she brought up one of her beloved animated movies from when she was little, a princess story that always comforted her when she was feeling down. That helped the time go by.

Just as the movie was ending, her phone chimed. It was a text from Max. **r u ok?**

Joy looked at the letters on the screen. Max was her closest friend. They texted every day. Today, though, she didn't know how to answer.

She glanced at the clock. It was eleven thirty a.m., the time they met at their usual table for lunch. With their class schedules, that was usually the first time they met during the school day, so maybe Max just wanted to know where she was. As if on cue, another text popped up. **where are u?**

Joy started thumb-typing. **At home.** She searched for what to say next, then added, **My mom called me in sick.**

r u sick?

For a second Joy hovered on the edge of silencing her phone, sticking it under a pillow, and going and hiding under the bed. But then she felt a slow, steady toughening-up inside her, just like when she had tried out for the cheer team. Mom was right. There were ways to fight. And if she was out at school, it was maybe going to be horrible for a while, but maybe not, and in any case, Max was her closest friend, and she was going to have to have the conversation sooner or later. It might as well be now. **Call me,** she texted.

Her phone rang, and she answered. "Hey, rock

star." That was Max's usual greeting since they'd started the Sparkle Squad.

"Hi, goat."

"So, what's up with you?"

Joy held the phone away from her ear for a second, not sure if she could go on. Max's tinny voice said, "Joy, are you there?"

Joy put the phone back to her ear. She could hear the racket of lunch in the background. "Max, I have something to tell you."

"Is it that you're trans?"

Joy gasped. "Why do you ask that?"

"Oh, well, you see, there's this rumor going around today, and I wondered if it might be true."

"Is that it? The rumor? Just that I'm trans?"

"No," Max said. "I also heard you'd been kicked off the cheer team."

Joy felt the grief and outrage rising up inside her again, but she forced herself to say as calmly as she could, "Yes it's true, they did that. That's what they say anyway."

"Because they think you're trans."

Joy held the phone away from her ear again. She was coming out, she suddenly realized. She hadn't planned to do this for years, or maybe ever, if that could somehow be managed, but now she was, and she was doing it now, to Max, her best friend in the whole world. She put the phone back and heard Max breathing, waiting silently for her answer. Joy took a long, slow, steady breath. "Not because they think I am, no." She hesitated for the briefest moment more, and then, visualizing her friend's kind, open face, took the plunge. "It's because I am. I am a transgender girl."

Over the line came the sound of lunch in the distance. Then her friend said, "That's stupid. They can't do that."

It took Joy a second to answer, because she had been expecting some reaction to the trans news. "But they say they can. There's this law, I guess. Um, did you hear what I said? That I'm trans?"

"Yeah, I heard you."

"And you know what that means, right?"

"I think I do. It's like they thought you were a boy when you were born, but they got it wrong. Is that it?"

"Pretty much, yeah." Joy paused. "Does that . . . I don't know, surprise you at all? Bother you?"

"No. Why, should it?"

"It's just that . . . so many people seem to think

it's such a big deal . . . I was expecting more of a . . . you know, you're actually the first person I've ever come out to . . ."

"It's all Gucci, Joy. You're, like, my best friend."

Joy felt a rush of affection. "Thank you," she said in a heartfelt tone.

"For what?"

"For being you. It means a lot to me that your first choice is to accept me the way I am." Saying these words, Joy felt how true they were. It was such a simple thing, but so powerful, that her friend had immediately rolled with her news.

"So you stayed home because you were upset?"

"Partly. But also because I don't know who knows. Until today it was only Principal Davis and a couple of teachers. And the nurse." Joy swallowed hard. "But I guess now . . . who told you the rumor? Who knows?"

"Whitney told me." Whitney was an eighth-grade girl on the cheer team who Joy didn't like at all. She was one of the most popular girls in school, and she acted like she was the boss of the whole team, and she loved gossip. "So maybe it's just in cheer."

"Maybe," Joy said, "but if Whitney is talking about it, I bet everyone is."

"You're probably right." There was a silence as the two friends thought about what that meant. Max asked, "What are you going to do tomorrow?"

Joy nodded, feeling that new strength still, like a bar of steel inside her. "I'm going to show up and be who I am," she said in a steady voice. "And I guess whatever happens, happens."

"That sounds scary to me."

"Me too. But what other choice do I have?" Outside, Joy heard the familiar sound of her mother's red Subaru pulling into the driveway. "I have to go," she said. "My mom is home."

"K, bye, rock star," Max said. "See you tomorrow."

"See ya."

eight

JOY RAN TO meet her mother at the door, equal parts eager and afraid to hear her news. They hugged, and Joy looked up into her mother's face, which seemed thoughtful and sad. That was pretty much her usual expression, though, so it was hard to guess what it might mean. "What did he say?" Joy asked.

Mom shook her head. "Some not very pleasant things. Let's get lunch ready, and when we've both had a bite to eat, then we can talk."

Joy opened her mouth to object, and Mom said gently, "Joy, I know it's hard to wait, but this will go so much better if you give me a chance to eat and think a little more first."

Joy nodded.

"How about if you help me get lunch ready? Then the talk can happen sooner."

Even though Joy wasn't really out sick, they made the usual out-sick lunch, which was tomato soup and open-faced toasted cheese sandwiches. It was a meal that made Joy feel safe and loved. All the same, her patience was dwindling. *What did the principal say?*

Mom finally put down her spoon and said, "Well. I suppose it could have been worse, but it isn't good. He confirmed that you are not going to be allowed to be on the cheer team."

Joy tried to match her mother's even tone. "I don't understand. When you met with him the first time, about living in stealth, it seemed like he was accepting."

"I've been thinking about that too, and what I'm realizing is, maybe we thought he was more supportive than he actually is. I was so nervous that he would be hostile, and he wasn't, but now that I think back, he wasn't exactly excited to have a trans girl in his school either. He said most of the right things, but more because he was obliged to. And now he says his hands are tied, because the order has come down from the superintendent's office." Mom reached out and took Joy's hand. "But I'm afraid that's not all. There's more bad news."

"What?" Joy was finding it harder to keep her voice steady.

"Mr. Davis also said, you can't use the girls' locker room anymore, and you're going to have to use the nurse's bathroom instead of the regular girls' room."

Joy felt tears prickling in the corners of her eyes. "Can they do that? Is there a law about that too?"

"I don't know about the law. That's a good question. But they can do whatever they want, really, at least in the short term. They run the school, so they make the rules." Joy burst into fresh tears. She had this horrible feeling like the world had judged her without actually knowing anything about her at all. The feeling made her want to crawl into bed with her stuffed animals and pull the covers over her head. Her mother scooched her chair around to comfort her.

Joy had been using girls' bathrooms her whole life, and up until now there had never been any issue. She knew to respect other people's privacy. She avoided eye contact and didn't speak to anyone.

She also valued her own privacy and always felt glad for the safety of a closed stall. From time to time she worried that other people in the bathroom were giving her funny looks, so she didn't always feel 100 percent safe, but so far nothing bad had happened to her.

Locker rooms had not been a problem in primary school, because there weren't any. At the start of the sixth-grade year, back in Minnesota, Mom had offered to write a note to get Joy out of PE, but Joy loved PE, so Joy had suggested adding changing in a stall to the strategy that they had used all along of careful clothing choices, and so far that had been working fine. It had turned out that she wasn't the only girl in either school who was shy about other kids seeing her body, so no one seemed to notice or care.

Mom let Joy cry for a minute, then took her daughter's chin in her hand and lifted her face up so they were looking in each other's eyes. "Joy, listen. I love you, and it's my job to protect you. This is unfair and unjust. You have just as much right to cheer on that team as any other girl. We can fight back against this."

"But how?"

"There are several things we can try. We can write a letter to the superintendent. And we can go to the next meeting of the school board and try to get them to change their minds there." Mom went back to eating. "Also, I did a quick search in the parking lot after meeting with Mr. Davis, and there's an organization called the Lone Star Rainbow Coalition that fights for the rights of LGBTQIA+ people in Texas. We can give them a call." Joy nodded, starting to feel a little better. She picked up her sandwich and took a bite. "Since you're home for the day, maybe you could do a little searching online too, and see who else might be able to help us."

"Really?" Joy said, surprised and pleased. Mom didn't usually allow free web browsing when she wasn't there. And it felt good to have something to do, instead of just sitting around feeling like the whole world was against her.

nine

AFTER MOM WENT back to work, Joy got one of her sketchbooks and a gel pen, opened the family laptop, pulled up a search screen, and stared at the blinking cursor. What should she search for? How about "Texas transgender kids sports"? She typed and hit return. The result was a bunch of news articles about the law that Principal Davis had talked about. She opened one and read enough to see that what Mom had said was right. The governor had signed a law saying that trans kids in Texas had to play on the team that matched the sex they were assigned at birth.

Joy made a snarl-face at the screen. Suddenly curious what this governor looked like, so she could understand who she was fixing to fight against, she switched over to videos and searched again, but she didn't see anyone who looked like a governor in the first few preview boxes. What she did see, in the third video frame down, was a little blond girl staring out of the screen at her. The title of the video was "Kai Shappley: A Trans Girl Growing Up in Texas." Intrigued, Joy clicked play.

The video was a mini-documentary about Kai's life, and Joy was not prepared for how deeply Kai's story resonated with her. Here was an adorable and smart six-year-old, who, just like Joy, had started telling the world as soon as she could that she was a girl. Kai's mom, Kimberly, had been a very conservative person who actually was a preacher in a megachurch, and at first she had tried to force Kai to be a boy, but Kai kept on insisting. It was a battle of wills, and finally it got so bad that one day when Kai was four, Kimberly overheard her praying to go home to Jesus rather than have to live one more day as a boy. That was when Kimberly started to change her mind.

There was another part of the documentary that was about the superintendent of Kai's school deciding that Kai had to use the boys' restroom. It was exactly like what had just happened to Joy.

Clearly, she and Kai had a lot in common. Kai had ended up using a nurse's bathroom, just like Joy had just been told she had to use, but sometimes the door was locked, so she had had accidents in the hall. The interviewer asked six-year-old Kai, "And how do you feel when you have accidents?" and six-year-old Kai said simply, "I feel embarrassed." Then she added, "And it wasn't my fault. It was the principal's boss's fault. Not mine. Because other girls get to go to the girls' bathroom, and I don't get to. And I'm a girl, so I should go to the girls' bathroom."

Joy found herself suddenly close to tears. She had clicked out of idle curiosity, but she had stumbled on what she least expected—proof that she was not alone in her new trouble. And Kai was amazing. She had such a natural way of looking at the camera and saying her truth. Joy was deeply impressed.

She took a closer look at the information about the video. It had been watched millions of times. Also, it had been posted five years ago, which meant that Kai was five years older now, which made her basically the same age as Joy. This meant that they had even more in common.

Joy did another search on Kai's name and discovered that she had her own channel with a lot of videos and a lot of followers. One title caught her eye: "Testifying Before the Texas Senate."

Joy clicked play and watched the two-minute video. Kai was older in this one, and she was in an echoey room with lots of dark wood and brass, reading something off her phone. Joy didn't understand exactly what was happening, but it seemed like maybe someone wanted to make a law that would hurt Kai's mom—maybe take away her nursing license for taking care of Kai?—and Kai was asking them to stop.

Kai started by saying a little about herself, including that she loved math—so there was one thing they did *not* have in common—and her cats and chickens. She mentioned that she wanted to meet Dolly Parton someday. Then her tone shifted from playful to serious. "I do not like spending my free time asking adults to make good choices. I have been having to explain myself since I was three or four years old. Texas legislators have been attacking me since pre-K. I'm in fourth grade now. When it comes to bills that target trans youth, I immediately feel angry. It's been very scary and overwhelming. It makes me sad that some politicians use trans kids like me to get votes from people who hate me just because I exist. God made me, God loves me for who I am, and God does not make mistakes."

All of this was amazing, but the best part was at the end, when Kai finished her testimony. There was some clapping in the room, and Kai smiled. Then a man's voice said, in the smarmy tone that some adults used to talk to little kids—Joy hated that tone—"Thank you for your testimony, Kai, thank you for being here. And do we have any questions for Kai?"

For a few seconds, Kai looked around the room with an expectant smile on her face, but no one said anything. "All right," the man said, but Kai talked over him.

"Seriously, none of y'all wanna know more about me?" This got a laugh from the people who had been clapping before, and from Joy too. It was awesome how confidently Kai talked to this roomful of important grown-ups. Joy felt starstruck. She was going to show this to Mom as soon as she got home.

Hey Jojo,

It's so unfair! Can't they see who I am? Can't they see how much I love cheer? It's the best thing in my life so far.

They're saying I can't use the girls' room anymore, even though I have been since school started, and I don't even know what's going to happen with PE. They're acting like I'm an alien or something. Do they really think I'm dangerous? I'm just a kid who loves cheer. I don't understand it all, and the whole thing has me shook.

But then Mom said we were going to fight, and she found some people who might help us, and when she came home from work, she said that one of them is coming to visit us on Saturday, a woman named Caroline. And besides that, I found my new idol, Kai Shappley, who is a trans girl in Texas just like me, fighting for her life. I showed Mom the video of Kai testifying, and Mom said that Kai was brave. Kai wants to meet Dolly Parton someday . . . and someday, I hope I'll get to meet Kai.

God bless Mom and Will and Max, who didn't even blink when I told her I'm trans, which, the more I think about it, the more amazing it is. She's such a good friend. And God bless Kai Shappley and all the other trans kids in the world, who just want to be themselves and live their lives without grown-up strangers trying to erase them from the world.

ten

"JOY."

"Go away."

"For the third time, Joy, you have to get up."

"I can't do it. Leave me alone."

"Sweetie, we're going to be late." Mom sat on the edge of the bed and tugged at the pillow Joy was holding clamped over her head. Joy yanked it back with a snarl. Mom sat in silence for a minute, then put a hand on Joy's arm. "All right, honey, if you truly think you can't face it, I'll give you one more day at home. One. But after that you're going to have to face what's happening. And, for what it's worth, I think you have what you need to survive this. You are strong. You are cheerleader strong."

Mom left. Joy lay still for a minute more. She

could feel her muscles wanting motion. Dread still hovered . . . but Mom was right. She had to face it sometime. She pushed through a final spike of fear and threw aside the covers.

Then she wished she had gotten up earlier, because she knew all eyes would be on her today, so she wanted to look her best, and now she had to rush through dressing. For lack of time, she fell back on a favorite blue skirt and a white cotton top with a lacy collar that she often wore to church, and tied her hair in a simple ponytail, while Mom fussed and jingled her keys. Breakfast was a hastily thrown-together peanut butter and jelly sandwich wrapped in a paper towel and eaten in the car.

Lying in bed the night before, Joy had imagined crowds of kids pointing and laughing, or yelling insults, or threatening to beat her up. But it wasn't like that at all. Mostly kids went by with the same elsewhere faces as always. As far as she could tell, nobody was paying any more attention to her than usual. So maybe the rumor hadn't spread far?

Then, when she was walking to her second-period class, she made eye contact down the hall with Whitney. The popular girl was walking with two friends, and when their eyes met, Whitney made a comment behind her hand to the two friends, and all three of them giggled. *Now it's starting*, Joy thought. But then second period was as normal as first period.

And so it went through the morning. Every once in a while, someone stared. A couple more times someone pointed and said something to someone else. Right before lunch, an invisible hand behind her knocked her books out of her arms as she approached her locker. She spun around to see who had done it, but whoever it was had already melted back into the crowd. Joy sighed, gathered up her scattered things, got her lunch out of her locker, and headed out to the Sparkle Squad's usual table.

Max was already there, smiling, as Joy sat down. "So you made it," she said, holding out her fist for a bump. "Gucci. Way to go, rock star."

"Hey, goat. Yep, I made it." But then Joy got stuck on her next sentence. She wanted to express how wonderful it had felt when her friend had instantly accepted her, but it seemed weird to just randomly say that at lunch. She thought of something that might work. "Thanks partly to you. I felt so much better after our call yesterday."

Max blushed a little and dropped her eyes, and Joy did an internal fist pump—compliment delivered.

They started to eat, just like any other day. Joy said, "Where's Steph?"

"I don't know. I haven't seen her yet today."

"I wonder if she knows."

"I don't know. Probably."

"I hope she's not going to be weird about it."

"Yeah, me too."

Another silence fell. Usually they talked about the cheer team, but that topic had been taken away from them. Joy hated feeling so awkward with her friend. Fortunately, Max came to the rescue by asking a question. "So, what are you going to do?"

"I don't know exactly yet, but Mom says we can fight it. Like, I'm going to write a letter to the superintendent. Also, someone is coming to visit us tomorrow who stands up against stuff like this all the time. She belongs to a group. Mom found her online."

"Gucci." They each took a bite. The awkward feeling was going away, thank goodness. Max said,

"But what I was actually asking about was, what are you going to do about cheer?"

"I can't do anything about cheer! That's the whole point!" Joy barked. Max looked hurt, and Joy said, "Sorry. I'm trying to stay calm, but I'm still so mad and upset. Not at you. At them, for kicking me off the team."

"I get it." Max took a sip from her thermos. "But you're going to keep practicing, right?"

"Why? What's the point?"

"Duh, the point is, you worked *really* hard all summer, and you have skills, Joy. If you don't keep them up, you'll start to lose them, and then you'll be behind when you win your fight and they have to let you back on the team."

Max's confidence made Joy smile. "I guess maybe you're right. . . . I should keep practicing."

"Heck yes, you should! You're just as much a cheerleader today as you were yesterday."

"That's right, I am. I'm getting to be a pretty good one, even. They can't take that away from me."

"That's right, they can't. You know what?" Max had just finished her sandwich, washing it down with a sip of the sweet tea in her thermos.

"What?"

"Let's practice right now."

"Now?"

"Yeah, out on the far field." That was what everyone at school called a big patch of open grass on the outer edge of the playground. "Let's go do some tumbling."

Joy gazed out past the climbing bars to the wide lawn beyond it. The idea of going on with cheer practice right in front of everyone made her breath catch in her throat. She could easily imagine it leading to more pointing and laughing, or insults, or worse.

On the other hand, it also felt like exactly the right thing to do. She needed to show her determination, not hide it away. "All right, let's do some tumbling."

As they got up, Max reached out a hand and shouted, "Yo, Steph!" Joy looked up and saw the third member of the Sparkle Squad standing several yards away. The way she was standing, it seemed like she had just turned to answer Max's call, which was weird, because normally she would have been walking toward them. "Hey, girl," Max called. "Wanna come tumble with us?"

Steph took a step sideways. Her face looked hard and closed, but that was how it always looked. She appeared to be arguing with herself. If she was, the argument ended with her suddenly walking toward them. When she was close enough, they were standing in a triangle. She looked Joy in the eye and went on to say some awful, uninformed things. Unfortunately, it wasn't the first time Joy had heard the words that came out of her mouth. Such words always hurt, but coming from someone she thought of as a friend, they hurt more. Steph's face was angry, scary, nothing like Joy had seen before.

"No," Joy said, feeling like she had been punched in the gut. "I am *not* a boy who dresses like a girl." All the different ways she and her mom had practiced talking to people about being trans came crowding into her head, and she stuttered. "I am a *girl*. A transgender girl . . . and there is absolutely nothing wrong with me."

Steph nodded, but not in a way that made Joy feel good about how the conversation was going. It was more like, in her own mind, Steph had just found out that things were as bad as she thought. When Steph spoke again, her voice was still hard and angry. "So you've been lying to us all this time."

"No! Not lying." Joy took a deep breath. "I've been keeping who I am a secret, because when people know, sometimes it's not safe for me."

Steph's expression showed she didn't believe this, if she had even heard it at all. "Well, I'm glad they kicked you off the team. And you're off the Sparkle Squad too. It's a girls-only team." She looked at Max as she said this, as if expecting her to agree.

That was not what happened.

Max looked back and forth between her two friends, standing glaring at each other. Her face showed how unhappy she was, but her mouth firmed up and she stepped to stand next to Joy, so that they faced Steph together. "Joy just said that she's a girl. And if anyone is off the Sparkle Squad, it's you, Steph."

Steph stared stone-faced at them both, then said between gritted teeth, "Fine. I don't want to be on your freak team anyway." She turned and walked away without looking back.

Hey Jojo,

It was so hard not going to cheer practice after school! I saw the other girls all going toward the gym, and I felt awful, all empty and full of pain inside. I wanted to wrap myself into a little ball and disappear. This sucks so bad.

Max is such a good friend. Not that I felt like going out and practicing tumbling after being called a freak. I went into the bathroom, after I remembered it had to be the nurse's bathroom, and cried, and then washed my face and went on to class. Next week, though, Max and I are going to practice every day after lunch on the far field.

Tomorrow morning this person Caroline is coming from the Lone Star Rainbow Coalition. I wonder what she'll be like.

God bless my best friend Max, and Mom and Will, and God bless Steph too, I guess, even if she can't see me for who I am.

eleven

A LITTLE BEFORE ten a.m., Joy parked herself on the couch below the front window so she could watch for Caroline Hayes's arrival. At precisely 9:59, a battered little hatchback pulled up to the curb, and their visitor got out and slammed the car door shut. She was a tall, broad-shouldered woman with dark brown skin and a majestic air about her. She was wearing a crisp skirt and blouse and strappy leather sandals. The lenses of her over-sized sunglasses reflected the sun. She carried a large purse on one arm, and she was wearing big fancy pearl earrings, a necklace, rings, and some bracelets too.

As she got nearer, Joy saw that her hair, which was full and fashionable, had a look to it that made Joy wonder if it might be a wig. Their visitor took off her sunglasses as she entered the shade of the porch, and Joy noted that her face was meticulously made up. She nodded with approval, recognizing skill when she saw it. She got up off the couch to go welcome their guest.

At first Ms. Hayes seemed a little intimidating, filling the small entryway inside the front door, but up close Joy could see that she had gentle, intelligent eyes with laugh crinkles at the corners. Mom said welcoming things, receiving a gracious thank you in return. Caroline Hayes's voice was quite deep, and Joy felt a thrill—it seemed obvious to her from all the clues that their visitor was a trans woman. Because she had always lived in stealth, Joy had only met a few other trans people in her whole life. This was exciting! Maybe she would get the chance to ask some questions.

Ms. Hayes shook hands with Mom and Will, who, to Joy's surprise, had asked if he could sit in on the meeting. Then she looked down at Joy and held out a hand. "Hello, young rainbow human," she said. "I'm delighted to make your acquaintance."

Joy smiled—she liked *rainbow human* a lot.

"Hello," she said. Their visitor's hand was large and warm. "Thank you for coming to talk with us today. I'm delighted to make your acquaintance too."

Their guest smiled a wide smile. Her teeth were a little crooked. "Well, now, isn't that sweet," she said. "You are quite polite. Nice and ladylike."

Joy felt her cheeks get warm. "Thank you, Ms. Hayes."

"Honey, you know what? How about if you call me Aunt Caroline instead?"

Joy glanced at her mother, who twisted her lips and rolled her eyes, as if to say, *Yeah, that's surprising, but go ahead if you want.*

"All right, thank you Ms. . . . Aunt Caroline."

Aunt Caroline laughed. "I guess you don't realize it yet," she said, "but you are going to start acquiring some new relatives now."

"I am?"

"Absolutely. Family of choice, you know. We rainbow humans have to stick together."

Mom offered lemonade and snacks. When they had settled in the living room, Aunt Caroline sitting in the big armchair with her legs elegantly crossed, she began to talk. "So, if I understand correctly from our phone conversation, Jenny, young Joy here has been living in stealth since y'all came to Texas. Do I remember right?"

"Yes, that's right," said Mom.

"And how has that been going, generally speaking?"

The three members of the Simmons family looked at each other. "It's been fine," Mom said. "We told the few people we had to at the school, but no one else knew."

"I'm glad to hear it. I do have to wonder why, having a trans child, y'all would choose to move to *this* state of all states."

Mom blushed a little, but said in an even voice, "I needed a new job quite badly, and I knew someone who had a lead."

"I see. I certainly understand about having to make hard choices. And before you moved here, what was Joy's life like?"

"It was much the same. Joy has always lived as a girl in the world. The ladies at the day care knew, but they were supportive. The town we lived in was more liberal than it is here."

"That sounds about as good as it could be," said Aunt Caroline. "Living the quiet life, all safe and in the closet. But things are going to change now."

"How?" asked Joy.

"Well, my dear, you are out now. You're going to meet people who think and sometimes say awful things about you, just because of what they think they know."

Joy thought of Steph and nodded.

"But on the flip side of that, as I already mentioned, you're going to start making some fabulous new friends too."

Now Joy thought of Kai Shappley, the activist she had seen in the viral video. Wouldn't *that* be amazing, if they could be friends? But Kai was famous, so it didn't seem possible.

"Beyond that," Aunt Caroline went on, "what happens depends on what y'all decide to do about the situation you find yourselves in."

"That's what I was hoping you'd talk to us about," said Mom. "This is still new for us. Can you tell us what our options are?"

"Of course," said Aunt Caroline, and then she talked at length, outlining paths forward from where they found themselves now. The choices ranged from meekly accepting being bumped off the cheer team (Joy scowled) up through writing a letter and going to school board meetings, as they were already planning to do, and then on to things like trying to make some noise about the ban online or staging a protest, and then all the way up to hiring a lawyer and suing the school.

"And I have to warn you," Aunt Caroline said, "the more you fight, the more hate you're going to get. But also, the more allies will come and join you."

To Joy's surprise, Will raised his hand. Aunt Caroline said, "Yes?"

Will said, "There's something I've been wondering about."

"Yes?"

"When they kicked Joy off the team, they said it was because she couldn't be on a girls' team. But what I was wondering is, is the cheer team actually only a team for girls? I mean, it's not like there's a boys' cheer team that she can be on instead."

Joy stared open-mouthed at her brother. Wild hope bloomed in her chest.

"Hmm, interesting," Aunt Caroline said. "But I would caution you against getting your hopes up. If this superintendent of yours is as determined as he seems to be, I would expect him to push back against that argument. Even if the team is for both girls and boys, he might say that if you want to be on it, you have to dress as a boy."

"I would never do that," Joy said.

"Of course you wouldn't, honey. It would be utterly absurd. But in my experience, that's the sort of logic our opponents bring to these fights. And, you must understand, if you decide to fight, it could be a long and difficult struggle. You want to be very sure before you start, because once you're in it, there's no way out except out the other end."

Hey Jojo,

I got a new aunt today, and she is awesome. At the end of her visit, I got my nerve up and asked her if she would tell us her story, and she said she was happy to. She has lived in Texas all her life, and she always knew she was trans, but she didn't transition until she was older than Mom. She lost almost all her hair before then, so she wears wigs, including one named Big Red. Well, sometimes she wears wigs and sometimes she doesn't. She says she feels fabulous either way. She's so, so nice, and she's going to help us fight against the superintendent.

Tomorrow after church I'm going to write my letter. Also, Mom did a search online, and it turns out that the school board meets next Tuesday, so I guess we're going to go to that. Aunt Caroline said we should take someone from her group with us, but it can't be her because she already has something that day, so she's going to send someone else instead, a man named Mac. I guess Aunt Caroline is right: we are going to make some new friends.

God bless Mom and Will and Aunt Caroline and Kai, and Max, and me too, please, since I'm asking for blessings. I don't usually ask for me too, but I could sure use a little extra blessing right around now.

Aunt Caroline!

twelve

FOR AS LONG as Joy could remember, the whole Simmons family had attended church almost every Sunday. Church was another thing that Joy cared about more than her mother and brother did. She loved everything about it—the connection with God, the feeling of community and belonging, the high-ceilinged sanctuary with its big sunny windows and the garden outside, the music and singing, getting to wear pretty dresses and shiny black shoes, and Reverend Elena Morales, a young woman with dark hair and intense eyes who preached with thrilling energy.

The Simmons' new church in Texas was what was called a welcoming and affirming congregation, which meant that LGBTQIA+ people were welcome to attend and be themselves. Joy found that comforting to know, even though nobody there knew that she was trans . . . or at least not yet. The little rainbow flag in the vestibule was a big reason Mom had chosen this church when they moved to the Houston suburbs. Mom seemed to like church in her quiet way, but to Joy it felt like her mother went more out of habit than because it was a big deal for her. In the last few months, Will had started saying he wanted to stay home, and Mom hadn't argued with him, so now it was just the two of them in the car each Sunday morning.

Reverend Morales seemed to have a magical ability to choose things to preach about that felt custom-made to help Joy with whatever problem she was dealing with. This magic didn't happen every week, but it did the day after Aunt Caroline's first visit. Of all the stories in the Bible Reverend Morales could have chosen to talk about, she chose the story of Esther.

Joy had heard the story of Esther before, of course, and at first she only listened with her usual dutiful attention. As the story unfolded, though, she found herself being drawn further and further in. Esther was a queen who dared to speak up, and because she was brave enough to do so, she saved her people from being killed. And, Reverend Morales went on to say, she was an example of how important it was for all of us to speak up when we saw injustice in the world, even if it might be dangerous for us to do so. By the time she said this part, Joy was so caught up in the sermon that she said "Yes!" out loud. People around her turned to look, and she blushed a little, but she wasn't sorry. It felt like, in that moment, God was speaking directly to her, telling her what she had to do.

In the car on the way home, Joy could still feel the energy from Reverend Morales's sermon vibrating inside her. She said to her mother, "I really liked the sermon today."

Mom, keeping her eyes on the road, nodded. "So did I, sweetheart."

"When we get home, I'm going to write my letter to the superintendent."

Now Mom glanced at her daughter for a moment. "That's a great idea, honey." Joy smiled. "And I've been thinking, with the school board meeting on Tuesday, we should probably deliver the letter by hand tomorrow, so we can be sure he gets it before the meeting." There was an unusual edge in Mom's usually quiet voice, and her hands were working and squeezing the steering wheel. Was Joy's gentle mother actually worked up? That hardly ever happened. Joy felt a thrill. She reached out and touched her mother's shoulder, receiving a glance and smile in return. "Mom?" she said.

"Yes, Joy?"

"I want to fight."

"So do I, honey. I think we have to." Mom's face went thoughtful. "Although, there is one thing I want to be careful about. When Aunt Caroline listed the things we could do, the one that made me worry was suing. That takes money, more than we have."

"But . . ."

"But, yes, everything else that Aunt Caroline said, we can do."

"Good."

"Maybe not all at once, but we'll get to it all if we have to." Mom signaled to turn into their street. "Speaking of Aunt Caroline's list, I remembered something during church. Your school has a parents' group online. I was invited to join it when we first moved here, but we had so much going on, it slipped my mind. Now, though, I think it would be useful to join, don't you?"

"Why?"

"Well, for example, we might find out who complained, or even how they found out."

Mom turned into their driveway. "And we might post something ourselves, you know. Get our version of the story out into the world, now that you've been outed."

"Sounds good to me." Joy unbuckled her seat belt. "Now, what are we having for lunch?"

thirteen

AFTER A TURKEY sandwich with kettle chips lunch with Mom and Will, Joy got her favorite purple pen from where it lay beside Jojo on her bedside table, sat down at her mother's little business desk, and looked at the blank sheet of sketchbook paper in front of her. She had no idea how to get started. Mom was in the kitchen, washing the lunch dishes. Joy called to her, "What should I write?"

Mom came and stood in the doorway, wiping her hands on a dish towel. "I'm not sure," she said. "This is still a new thing for us. But I guess maybe you can keep it simple. Tell him who you are and why you are writing, and then do your best to describe how being removed from the cheer team made you feel." Joy frowned. "What is it, sweetheart?"

"Do I really have to do that last part? I don't mind writing in my journal about how I'm feeling, but telling other people? People I don't even know?"

"I can see how that might be scary, but I think you should try. Maybe the idea is to try to get him to feel at least a little bit of what you're feeling."

"Get him to feel what I'm feeling . . ." Joy sighed and nodded. "Got it," she said, and Mom went back into the kitchen. Joy pondered another minute. The video she had watched of Kai Shappley's testimony came back into her mind, and she remembered other pictures of Kai from when she was searching, pictures in which she was wearing a rainbow tutu, or holding a trans flag, or wearing a T-shirt that said *Y'all Means All.* Kai was so strong and free, so joyfully herself, in her activism, and in her testimony video, she had done exactly what Mom had just said. That helped. She glanced at the sticky note Mom had written the superintendent's name on, then clicked her pen and wrote:

Dear Superintendent Fellows,

My name is Joy Simmons and I am twelve years old. I am in the seventh grade at Appleton East Middle School. I am the girl that you said couldn't be on the cheer team anymore, because I am transgender.

Mr. Fellows, have you ever met a transgender person? A lot of people have not. Maybe that is one of the reasons why people have such weird ideas about us. But I am just a regular girl, and I love cheer, so when Principal Davis said I couldn't cheer anymore, it made me very sad. What makes it even worse is, I added an idea to the new cheer for when we play Basswood in a couple of weeks. It breaks my heart that I might not be there, when I helped make up part of the cheer.

These rules are unfair. I'm a girl, so I should be allowed to do what other girls have the right to do. I am writing to ask you to undo these new rules and let me cheer and use the girls' bathroom and locker room just like I have since I started going to school at Appleton Middle.

Signed,

Joy Simmons

Joy read back through what she had written. She had no idea if it was any good or not. She took the letter into the kitchen. Mom and Will were both sitting at the dining table, Will on his phone, Mom on her laptop. Mom's eyebrows were bunched together as she clicked and scrolled.

"Mom, can I read this to you?"

"In a minute, honey," Mom said, still frowning at her screen.

"What's going on? Is something wrong?"

With an effort, Mom pulled her eyes away from her laptop. "Not wrong, exactly. That's not the word I would use. But I am . . . flummoxed, I guess would be a good word."

Curious, Joy stepped around the table, heading to take a look. Mom folded the computer screen shut. Joy stopped, surprised.

It was Will who spoke next. "Mom, no one cares if you play solitaire. It's nothing to be ashamed of."

Mom gave Will a quick eye roll. "It's not that."

"Then what?" said Joy.

Mom thought for a second, still holding the computer screen closed. Then she sighed and said, "I guess it's okay for you to see. It's nothing too bad, at least not yet. And Aunt Caroline did warn us." She opened her laptop again, and both of her children got behind her to look. "This is the Appleton East Middle School parents' group I told you I was going to check out. And it appears our news is spreading. There are several posts about you, Joy. Or at least, about what people think they know about you. And . . . well, not all of them are kind."

Joy could feel her heart beating faster than usual, but she was also very curious, and Mom was still holding the screen open, so she began to read. One person had written, *You mean to tell me they're letting boys compete on girls' teams now? That's just wrong.* Joy shook her head. That was not what had happened at all. She looked at the couple of comments that were visible under the post, and they agreed with the post.

The next post down said, *There's no way a kid that young is old enough to know they're trans. They are being indoctrinated by their parents.*

"What does 'indoctrinated' mean?" Joy asked.

Mom said, "It means the person who wrote that thinks I forced you to be a girl."

"But that's so wrong! It was exactly the opposite."

"I know, honey. You know, maybe you shouldn't

be reading these." Mom moved her hand to close the screen.

"Wait," said Will. "Look at the second comment down on that post." The comment he meant was just visible at the bottom of the page.

Mom scrolled down, and they all three read, *You don't know what you are talking about. Children as young as two already know. Trans girls are girls, period.*

"All right," Mom said, "we do also have some friends here. But that's enough. I don't want you getting upset." She closed the computer.

Joy opened her mouth to object, but then she realized that she was shaking and closed her mouth again. What was this feeling she was feeling? Was it fear? No, not really. Anger? Maybe a little. No, mostly, it was frustration. How could people be so sure about something they knew nothing about? She wanted to magically appear wherever the writers of those posts were and shout at them, *You don't know me at all!* But she couldn't.

"Did you want to read something to us?" Mom asked.

It took Joy a moment to change gears in her

mind. "Um, yes, right. It's my letter to the super-intendent."

"Go ahead." Joy looked at the paper in her hand and cleared her throat, suddenly feeling self-conscious. "You've got this, sweetheart," Mom said. "I'm sure it's fine."

fourteen

JOY READ THE letter. When she finished, she kept her eyes down. There was a short silence. Then Mom said, "Honey, it's great."

Joy looked up. "Really? You like it?"

Mom nodded.

Will had a weird expression on his face, and it took his little sister a second to realize he was smiling. That never happened. "It's really good," he said.

Joy gaped at him. She couldn't remember the last time he had given her a compliment. But he wasn't done surprising her. "You know what?" he said. "I have an idea. What if we made a video of you reading it and posted it on that forum?"

Joy felt an instant burst of excitement. If they

did that, she could be like Kai. She could speak out. And Will knew about how to make videos for the internet, because he had a gamer channel he was trying to get going. Before she could figure out what to say, though, Mom said, "I'm not sure that's a good idea."

"Mom!" Joy said.

"I don't know, honey. It doesn't feel safe."

Again, it was Will who spoke. It was like he was changing into a completely different brother. "But isn't this exactly what Ms. Hayes—I mean, Aunt Caroline—said? She said the more we do, the more hate we'll get, but the more friends and allies we'll get too."

"I suppose," Mom said, but she obviously wasn't convinced.

Joy stepped close and held her mother's arm. "Please, Mom. Will is right. This is it. It's what we talked about in the car. This is the beginning of the fight."

Both of the Simmons children watched their mother as she pondered these words. At last she sighed and pulled Joy into a hug. "All right, sweetie. I can see the fire in you. As your mom it scares me, but I guess maybe I'm just going to have to get used to that. Go ahead."

Joy squeezed her mother back. "Thank you," she whispered.

"You're welcome, honey."

Making a video with Will meant going into his room, which normally Joy would never have wanted to do. She didn't need the big *Keep Out* sign on the door to keep her away. Will's room was by far the messiest room in the house, cluttered and dim, with dirty laundry lying here and there on the floor and an unmade bed. At some point Mom had given up trying to get him to keep it neat. She had declared it his zone and given him control. The result, in Joy's mind, was a dingy, smelly boy-cave that made her skin crawl to enter. But this was too important, so she pushed through the shiver and made her way to his desk chair, being careful to touch as little as possible.

It got better once she was in the chair. Will knew what he was doing. Joy watched as he got a colorful bedsheet from the hall closet and thumbtacked it up so it covered his gaming and rock posters on the wall behind her. Then he turned a bright circular light in her direction. She blinked and squinted, and he said, "Try to get used to it if you can. It's important to be well lit."

So Joy practiced opening her eyes wide despite the glare. She also checked her hair, looking at the image of herself on the screen of Will's computer. "Why are you doing this?" she asked.

"Oh, I don't know," Will answered. "I guess I just think it's cool that you want to stand up for yourself."

Joy was surprised to find herself blushing. "Thanks," she said, really meaning it.

"You're welcome. Are you ready?"

"Yes, I guess."

"Two things. Don't look at yourself on screen, or else it'll look like you're looking away. Look right at the camera, here." He tapped a dark circle in the middle of the laptop's upper edge. "And the other thing is, take your time. There's no rush. Read nice and slow."

Joy nodded, accepting these instructions. "What if I mess up?"

"Then we can do it again, until we get it right. It's easy."

That was a relief to hear. "Okay."

"Look at the camera, and one, two, three, go,"

and on the word "go," Will tapped a key. A bright point of light appeared next to the dark camera circle, and Joy read her letter. She did her best to resist the temptation to look at herself, and she took her time. When she finished, Will tapped the keyboard again, and the little camera light turned off.

"Let's watch it," Will said, and they did. The girl on the screen, her from a few seconds ago, seemed serious and real. It was like seeing Kai testify. She felt excitement stirring inside her again. This was fun.

When they had watched to the end, Will looked at Joy, and she realized he was waiting to see what she thought. That felt good too. "I think it's good?" she said.

"Me too. It's really good." He smiled again. Two smiles in one day. Joy's world was changing. "I'll add a graphic at the beginning to say who you are, and then we can upload it."

Hey Jojo,

We are going to post the video Will helped me make tomorrow in the forum Mom found. I wanted to post it tonight, but Mom said that would mean I would stay up all night checking to see if there were any comments, and I had to wait. She said we could post it after dinner tomorrow.

When Mom said good night just now, she said she was proud of me, and she said, "Try not to be scared, honey." But you know what? I'm not scared. I feel brave. I don't know why, but I do, and I like it. Go me!

God bless Mom, and Will for his help with the video, and Max, and Kai, and Aunt Caroline, and everyone else who wrote things on the forum on our side. Mom said we could read a few more after dinner, and it was hard to see the mean and stupid things people were saying, but we found more on our side too. Will used the word "allies" for them, and it was about fifty-fifty. So, God bless all our allies too.

fifteen

FIRST STOP ON Monday morning was the superintendent's office. In the car, Joy chewed on her fingernails, which she tended to do when she was anxious. Mom told her twice to stop, but after a minute she was chewing again, until finally Mom reached over and gently pushed her hand away from her mouth. "Try not to worry," she said.

"But his rule is so mean," Joy said fretfully. "What if he's mean in person too?"

"I don't think that's going to happen. In fact, I bet we won't even get to meet Mr. Fellows this morning. In an office like this, there's usually a secretary or receptionist."

Joy was not convinced and was back to biting her nails by the time they pulled into the big parking lot, but her mother turned out to be right. They did not meet the superintendent. Once inside the building, they followed signs down a long hall to a door that opened into a room like a waiting room at a doctor's office. A woman with mounds of curly red hair and heavy makeup sat behind a desk. She gave them a smile when they came in and said, "Mornin'. May I help you?"

Mom nudged Joy forward, and Joy stepped up to the desk. "I have a letter for the superintendent," she said shyly.

"Well, now, bless your heart," the woman said brightly. "You can give it to me, and I'll make sure he gets it." She held out a hand with long, sparkly fingernails.

Joy handed her the letter, neatly sealed in an envelope with the superintendent's name written on it. "Thank you."

"You're welcome, darlin'," the woman said. She dropped the letter in a wire basket on her desk and gave them another big smile and said, "Y'all have a nice day now," but then the smile disappeared like a light being switched off, and the woman turned back to her computer. There was nothing left to do but leave.

In the car, Mom asked, "Joy, are you all right?"

Joy made an effort and said, "Sure, Mom, I'm fine," but she didn't feel fine. The big strange office building that they had just left had frightened her. How could one seventh-grade girl like her hope to fight against so much steel and glass? Her confidence was shaken.

They were a little late for school, so Joy checked in at the front office, then slipped quietly into the back of her first-period class. No one even looked at her. It didn't last, though. Between second and third periods she had two icky encounters, one after the other. The first was with Whitney and her posse, walking toward her down the hall. No one said anything, but the looks on the other girls' faces were the same as all of them yelling, *Freak!* and just as they passed, the whole group of them burst out laughing.

The second was with another girl on the cheer team, an eighth grader named Carmen, a tall girl with long black hair. Joy admired Carmen, because she was good at cheer, and because she really seemed to live the honor code. Carmen didn't have a posse, but she didn't need one to make Joy feel small. As they passed in the hall, the older girl gave Joy a long, slow look up and down, then frowned and turned her eyes coldly away. Joy felt judged and dismissed, and tears stung the corners of her eyes.

At lunch, Max said, "Joy, there's something I've been thinking about."

"What's up, goat?"

Max blushed and dropped her eyes. "I was wondering . . ."

Joy couldn't remember ever seeing her friend look bashful. "You were wondering . . . ?"

"I was wondering, what would you think if I quit the cheer team too? You know, in solidarity with you."

"Max! I don't want you to quit the team! You love it as much as I do!"

"Yeah, I know, but still."

Joy took both of Max's hands in her own. "Max, I love you for asking, but I would feel terrible if you quit too. I would feel like the haters had won."

"Are you sure? Because I'm so disgusted, part of me just wants to do it."

Joy stared into her friend's eyes. "I'm absolutely sure. Thank you, bless you, for asking, but no."

They smiled at each other. "And anyway, how will I know what's going on if you don't spy for me?" Joy added, and they both laughed.

After lunch they headed out to their spot and did some stretches and tumbling. Max's generous offer had erased Joy's bad mood, and it felt good to be moving her body. All the same, it was lonely out there in all that green, and every other minute Joy found herself looking back toward the main part of the playground, scanning for staring eyes and pointing fingers.

In the afternoon between classes, Joy found herself face-to-face in the hall with a kid she knew only a little, a boy with messy long hair, jeans with holes at the knees, and a band T-shirt so old it was hard to read which band it was. He sat at the gamer table in the cafeteria, mostly, Joy recalled. What was his name? Todd? That might be right. Whoever he was, he was looking at her oddly. She opened her mouth to ask what he wanted, but he got there first.

"I—I—I just wanted to tell you, Joy, I support you," he said. Then he blushed, dropped his eyes, and hurried away. He moved so fast that he was almost out of earshot before Joy could thank him.

By the time school let out, Joy felt drained. It was hard, being on constant alert, always braced for random nastiness. Or for awkward kindness, though of course that wasn't as bad. It was still work, though, having to be ready to respond to anything at any time. Hoping to avoid meeting anyone else, she decided to slip out the side door, rather than the crowded front, and made her way home. Her nails were ragged from a day of chewing, and a couple of them were torn so short that the soft red skin that was usually underneath the nail twinged when she touched anything.

sixteen

AS THE TIME for posting the video got closer, the scornful words and wrong ideas people had written about her echoed in Joy's head. When she was setting the table, Viking suddenly barked at a crow he saw through the sliding glass doors, and Joy dropped a glass. Luckily, it bounced on the carpet and didn't break.

Mom heard, though, and came to help Joy finish her task. "Honey, what's going on with you?" she asked gently, setting out trivets for hot serving bowls. "You seem jumpy."

"I'm not sure what's going to happen when we post the video."

"Yes, I've been thinking about that too. It's going to be important for us, going forward, to learn how to handle what people say. But that's not the only thing."

Joy gulped. "There's something else?"

"Yes, there is. So far we haven't known who knows and who doesn't know. But after this, everyone will know."

Joy stood still to think about this. "You're right." The idea was good for a shiver.

Mom stepped around the table and pulled Joy close. "I think it's actually a good thing," she said. "It's been stressful not knowing who knows." Joy, leaning into her mother's solid warmth, nodded. "But once we post the video, we can assume that everyone does. And you know what? It might be easier that way."

Joy nodded again, feeling a little better. She was going to be like Kai Shappley, out and proud for everyone to see. And she was happy to notice that although she still felt nervous, she felt excited too. It was like the moment when she had tried out for the cheer team and had realized that she could do it. She laughed a little and said, "I hope I can eat."

Mom laughed too. "I feel you. But it's mac and cheese, your favorite."

"With green peas?"

"Of course with green peas. I know what my girl likes. Oh, and one more thing—it might be a good idea for us to send your video to Aunt Caroline. I bet she'd like to see it."

"That's a good idea," Joy said, thinking how good it would make her feel if Aunt Caroline liked what she had done.

Joy ate with a good appetite, and when the dishes were washed and the kitchen was tidied, all three members of the Simmons family gathered around the family laptop on the dining room table. Joy and Will watched as Mom uploaded the video to the parents' group and then typed underneath it, *This is my daughter, Joy Simmons, who has something she wants to say.* Then she hovered her finger over the enter key and said, "Are you ready? Once I press this button, there's no going back. We're coming out as a whole family, right now."

Joy's nerves spiked, and she made a little *eep!* sound. "Do it, do it!" she said. "Before I chicken out." Mom pressed enter. The post appeared at the top of the chain of posts.

Seconds ticked by. Nothing happened. Then

Will pointed and said, "Look." Down in the corner of the video frame, there was a little view counter. It had just switched from *0 views* to *1 view*. As they looked at it, it switched again to *2 views*.

"People are watching it," Joy whispered. Mom gave her an encouraging smile. On the screen, the counter switched to *3 views*. The likes counter switched from zero to one, then a second later to two. The bouncy-dots graphic for someone typing a comment appeared on the screen, and all three leaned closer. The comment appeared: *LOL!* it said, with a laugh-cry emoji.

"Steady," Mom said. "Remember, it's going to be a mix of good and bad."

Another comment appeared: *Good job*, it said. Now the video had four likes.

"There, see?" said Mom.

"Can we answer some of them?" Joy asked. "The ones who get it wrong?"

Mom shook her head. "We will not be answering any of these, not yet. I will not debate your right to exist in the world with ignorant strangers."

Joy would have kept watching all night if she had been allowed. When Mom said it was time for homework, Joy waved an impatient hand at her, then squawked when Mom started to close the laptop. That got her the Mom-look with the frown line between the eyes. "Joy Simmons, if you cannot handle this, I will not let you look at all."

Joy opened her mouth to argue, but Mom held up a warning finger. "I'm serious. This is not going to take over our lives. We still have all our regular living to do."

"But, but . . ."

"No debate. We can look one more time, together, before bed, but after that, not again until morning."

For a moment mother and daughter stared at each other. Then Joy said reluctantly, "Okay, Mom," and watched as her mother closed the screen. It took her a minute to get started on her homework—most of her brain was still in the parents' forum—but then she took a deep breath and started wrestling with the first math problem on the worksheet in front of her. Mom pressed a loving hand on the back of her daughter's neck for a second, then sat down on the couch with a book.

Hey Jojo,

A minute ago my video had been watched sixty-three times, with thirty likes. Mom thinks we found out who complained about me being on the cheer team, because the person said so in a reply. It was Mrs. Abernathy, Carmen's mom. She wrote, "I did what I had to do to protect our girls," which is stupid and wrong, seeing as how I'm a girl too, and not dangerous to anyone. At least somebody else replied to her reply and said so.

It's just like the first time—there are some people against us, and some people on our side. Mom said we can check again in the morning, but no getting up at night to look, and then she unplugged the laptop and took it with her into her room. I don't think she had to do that. I wouldn't have looked in the night. Well, not more than a couple of times. I can't look at it on my phone because Mom is in the group, not me.

I wonder what school will be like tomorrow, but I hope not worse than today. And then tomorrow night we're going to the school board meeting.

God bless Mom and Will, and Max, and everyone who posted nice comments or replies for my video. I'm out! Mom was right, it's a relief.

seventeen

BY MORNING THE video had more views, likes, and comments, but not a lot more, and Mom was firm about Joy taking only one quick look, then getting ready for school and arriving there on time. The comments were still split just about fifty-fifty between nice and mean. In the car on the way to school, Joy fumed a little. She still wanted to be watching the post in real time. She had no way to do it, though. Now she had to show up at school and deal with pointing fingers and stares and mean remarks.

There were a few more smirks and laughs from people passing, and a few more incidents of people pointing and staring. Mostly, though, the other kids ignored her. In a way, still feeling jazzed about the video, she almost felt annoyed about that. But then Steph walked by her in the hall and gave her an icy glare, and that helped her remember that there were real people behind all the reactions, including the bad ones. She had just started to feel like Steph was a real friend right before she was outed, and now her former "friend" clearly hated her. That hurt.

There were also a few other kids, kids she didn't even know, who made eye contact and nodded, or who smiled shyly and then looked away. Joy coached herself to try to respond in real time, nodding or smiling back.

After lunch, when Joy and Max went out to the far field, they started out there alone, but after a while another girl from the cheer team wandered by in an accidentally-on-purpose sort of way and stopped to watch while Joy and Max worked on their back walkovers. Joy glanced at her a couple of times, but the girl's face was hard to read. Was she judging, or curious, or just shy? In practice she had always been one of the girls who kept to herself and didn't say much.

Joy decided to be bold. "Hi," she said. "Theresa, right?" The other girl nodded. "We're practicing," Joy went on. "Do you want to take a turn?"

Theresa looked around, toward where most of the other kids were playing, then back at the two remaining members of the Sparkle Squad. "Really?"

"Really," said Max, in her usual friendly, open way. "You're welcome to join us." So then for the rest of lunch recess it was three girls, not two, practicing their tumbling close to the school's back fence.

As soon as Joy got home from school, she opened the laptop to see how many more likes and comments her video had gotten, and was surprised to see there were only a few more than in the morning. Will happened to pass by and glance over her shoulder at that moment and heard the disappointed sound she made. "What's up?" he asked.

She pointed at the numbers. "They haven't changed hardly at all."

"That's not surprising. When I post my videos, I get all my reactions in the first day, mostly. The internet has a really short attention span." Joy made a frustrated sound, and Will said, "Why does it matter so much to you? I mean, it's nice to get likes, sure, but you seem weirdly intense about it."

"It's just . . ."

"What?"

"It's just, the Basswood game is in less than two weeks, and the team is doing my choreo, and I have to be there. I have to be back on the team by then."

"Oh." Will frowned.

"What?"

"I guess, don't get your hopes up too high."

"Why not?"

"It's just, from what we've seen so far, I don't know if this superintendent is going to change his mind."

Joy didn't want to think about that, so she went back to reading comments. As she had the evening before, she found herself wanting to answer some of the worst ones, but Mom's tone of voice and face when she had said no to that were still fresh in her mind, so she kept her hands in her lap.

The plan for the evening was to have an early

dinner, then wait for the arrival of Aunt Caroline's friend Mac Jameson from the Rainbow Coalition, who was coming to help them at the school board meeting.

eighteen

BY FIVE FORTY-FIVE p.m. Joy found herself camped out on the couch, trying to tame the butterflies in her stomach. She was excited to meet this new person, and nervous and excited about going to confront the superintendent face-to-face. In her keyed-up state she started chanting a little under her breath. "Rainbow kids deserve to live," she began, and then noticed that it sounded a little like the start of a cheer. It had that certain rhythm to it. What would the next line be? How about, "The same as everybody else." Hmm, maybe? It didn't rhyme. But did it have to rhyme? She thought about the cheers she had already learned. Some rhymed and some didn't. Maybe she was onto something here. She could start writing her own cheers. The idea made her feel warm all over—it was the first time she had felt completely good about cheer since being kicked off the team.

A few minutes before six, a mud-spattered blue Jeep pulled up by the mailbox, and a man got out. He was short and quite broad in the body, with a barrel chest and bandy legs. He was wearing khaki shorts and had large, hairy calves showing above the tops of the mismatched socks that poked up out of his white athletic shoes. He was also wearing a polo shirt, a bill cap, and silver sunglasses, which he took off and stuck up on the visor of his cap as he came clomping up the walk. Joy jumped up to answer the door.

Up close Mac Jameson had stubbly cheeks, sparkly intelligent eyes, and an easy grin. His voice when he said hello turned out to be a reedy tenor, and Joy began to wonder—could this Mac person possibly be a trans man? It would hardly be surprising, but it was not easy to know for sure. As far as she knew, Joy had only met one out trans man so far. Travis had been the leader of a support group she had visited a couple of times back in Minnesota, and he had looked quite different— a slim, small man with a little mustache.

She didn't have to wonder long. After greetings were exchanged, their visitor said, "Caroline has told me about you, and I'm excited to meet y'all. We trans folk need new young voices like yours so badly right now. So, welcome to the tribe and to the struggle!"

"Thank you, Mr. Jameson," Joy said.

"Please, call me Mac," he said with a grin. *How about Uncle Mac?* Joy thought, but didn't say. She didn't have to. "Or Uncle Mac, if you'd like," he went on, and looked startled when the whole Simmons family burst out laughing.

Before he could take offense, Mom hurried to say, "We're laughing because as soon as she came in, Caroline said more or less exactly the same thing."

Uncle Mac laughed too. "That's awesome," he said. "I'm happy to join your rainbow family."

Mom offered their guest sweet tea and cookies, but he politely declined. "I've got my water bottle," he said, holding it up. "And we don't have much time. It's important to get to school board meetings early, because often they have a sign-up sheet to speak, and you never know when sign-ups will be cut off."

Mom and Joy exchanged a glance. "So much to

learn," Mom said, and Joy nodded. It was helpful to have allies, especially allies who had been in the fight for a while and knew what to do.

"Don't worry, I'll take good care of you," Uncle Mac said. "But we should get going. We can talk in the car."

As Mom drove to the high school where the meeting was being held, Mom and Mac in front and Joy in back, Mac offered more coaching. Besides making sure to sign up on time, he also suggested that it was important to always be polite and courteous, even if people said ignorant or hurtful things. He also said, keep it short. "I watch in meetings all the time when people get up to speak, and the people who are supposed to be listening start looking at their phones or computers after about two minutes." He also said that it was good to make it personal, to tell your real story and try to get people to see you as a person like them. "Like your video," he said to Joy. "Caroline shared it with me, and you did a really nice job on that."

"Thank you," Joy said, glowing. She thought of Will. "It was my brother's idea, and he shot it, too." Mom glanced back to give her a smile and a nod.

"Well, then, you and Will did a good job, and you can tell him I said so."

The meeting was in a school gym. The members of the board were sitting up on the stage at tables with microphones on them. Down on the floor there were chairs set out in rows, with a podium at the front where people could step up to talk. There were only about fifteen people in the room.

There was a clipboard on a table outside the door, with a form to write your name if you wanted to talk. Mom added her name underneath one other name. She also picked up a handout with the agenda. The open comments part of the meeting was at the very end, after the board had done all its other business.

"Yeah, I know, it's a pain," said Uncle Mac. "Showing up at meetings can mean a lot of waiting."

While different speakers droned on about budgets and contracts, Joy took the opportunity to study the face of Superintendent Fellows. It was a heavy, unmoving face. He looked like a man who had disapproved of so many things his whole life long that disapproval had become his default expression. She tried to imagine him smiling, and couldn't do it. Minutes dragged by. Joy took out her phone and played a game with the sound off. Mom tapped Joy on the leg to get her to stop kicking the chair in front of her. More minutes dragged by.

Finally, over an hour after the start of the meeting, open comments were announced. Joy perked up. The other person who had signed up was a woman who had a complaint about her son unjustly getting in trouble. Her story wandered confusingly, but the people on the stage listened patiently. When she was done, the woman with the clipboard called, "Jennifer Simmons."

nineteen

MOM GAVE JOY a quick leg-squeeze and a smile, then stood up and stepped to the podium. The people up on the stage, sitting at the folding tables, stared at her with blank faces. Besides the superintendent, there were six other people on the stage. When she reached the podium, Mom cleared her throat, and the amplified sound of it made her flinch back a little from the microphone. "Excuse me," she said. On the stage, nobody moved. Mom looked up at them for a second longer, then began to speak.

"Good evening," she said, in the quiet, even tone that Joy thought of as her library voice. "My name is Jennifer Simmons, and my daughter is Joy Simmons." Mom glanced back at Joy, and Joy saw the eyes in the faces up on stage shift to look at her. She blinked in surprise at the sudden attention, but made herself look back. "I'm here this evening to follow up on a letter that Joy and I hand-delivered yesterday to your office, sir," Mom went on, nodding at Superintendent Fellows. "It was a letter from Joy expressing her sadness that you made the decision that she can no longer participate on the Appleton East Middle School cheer team." The superintendent was sitting as still as a statue. Mom faltered a moment, then said, "May I ask, sir, did you receive the letter?"

Mr. Fellows leaned slightly forward toward his microphone and said, "I received the letter."

"And have you read it?" Mom asked.

The superintendent's face went sour. "I read it."

"Good. So you know now that your arbitrary decision to remove my daughter from the cheer team based on her gender identity has negatively impacted her. Of all the things your school has to offer, she loves cheer the most. It is the center of her educational experience."

Silence fell. Joy realized that Uncle Mac, sitting next to her, was filming on his phone. He had the camera zoomed in on Superintendent Fellows's face. Mr. Fellows worked his mouth like he had just taken a bite of something that had gone bad in the fridge. Then he said, "There is no place on a girls' cheerleading team for your son."

A murmur passed through the room. Mom stepped back from the podium for a moment, but then she approached the microphone again and said clearly, "Please show some respect, sir. Joy is not my son, and it is presumptuous and rude for you to say that she is. She is my daughter. My transgender daughter."

Mr. Fellows scowled. Another silence stretched out. Mom glanced back again, and Joy could see that she was not sure what to do next. At Joy's side, Uncle Mac gave her a thumbs-up and a nod. Mom turned back and said, a little less calmly now, "Actually, I'm glad you said what you said, because I wanted to ask: Is the cheerleading team in fact just a girls' team? If there's a separate boys' team, I'm not aware of it." Joy thought, *We have to make sure to tell Will.*

The other people up on the stage had joined the rest of the room in watching the superintendent. Mr. Fellows said in a cold, grating voice, "That's not the issue. The issue is, the Appleton School District does not support you in your attempts to indoctrinate your child into your perverted lifestyle." Joy thought to herself, *There's that word "indoctrinate" again. And what's that other word, "perverted"?* She had heard it before, but she wasn't sure what it meant.

Mom gasped. "That's preposterous," she said sharply, and the superintendent scowled harder and reached for the little wooden hammer he had banged on the table to start the meeting. Mom made a visible effort to calm herself and tried again. "With all due respect, sir," she said, "that is a gross mischaracterization of our family's situation. Nobody is indoctrinating anyone. And—"

Before she could say more, Mr. Fellows banged the hammer on the table, looked at the woman with the clipboard, and said loudly, "Is there anyone else signed up to speak?"

Mom tried to start another sentence, but Mr. Fellows ignored her completely, and she stammered to a halt. The woman with the clipboard, her eyes wide, shook her head no, and the superintendent banged his hammer again.

"Meeting adjourned," he said, and then he immediately got up, walked off the stage, and left the room.

When Mom came back to her seat, she was shaking. Joy had only seen her normally mild mother get angry a few times, and it always made an impression on her. "How dare he." Mom's voice was shaking, too. "What a horrible thing to say."

Uncle Mac nodded and said, "But not surprising. Nothing happened here tonight that we haven't seen and heard somewhere else already."

"And then just leaving like that," Mom said. "So rude!"

"Yep. But, Jenny, you did great. Just the right amount of pushback, without forgetting to be courteous. I got some good footage that we can maybe use if we need to."

At this point their discussion was interrupted by the arrival of a young man with bright, curious eyes who was holding a small notebook and a pen. "Excuse me," he said. "My name is Evan Olson, and I'm a reporter with Houston Online. May I ask you a couple of questions?"

Mom glanced uncertainly at Uncle Mac, who smiled and nodded.

"All right," Mom said. "Ask away."

Hey Jojo,

Tonight the superintendent said that me being the way I am is a "perverted lifestyle." I asked Mom in the car what "perverted" meant. She said it was a word grown-ups use for things they think are naughty or nasty in a particular grown-up way. That's terrible! There's nothing naughty or nasty about me. I am the way I am, and I always have been, and it's totally fine and normal. At least it would be if people like him would stop saying awful things about me, when they don't even know what they're talking about. And saying Mom was making me do it, too! When I was the one who had to make her do it, so that I could live my life and be a real person in the world.

Jojo, I have to tell you, the superintendent scared me a little. He was big and loud, and his face and voice were so hard, and he seemed like a person who never listens to anyone but himself. I don't know how to fight someone like that. I don't know how to even say any-thing that he can hear at all. Yuck. I had to take a hot shower when I got home. I felt like someone had thrown slimy, sticky mud on me.

At least we got to meet Uncle Mac, who I like a lot. He said we'll probably see him again, unless we decide to stop fighting, but how can we do that now? We have to keep fighting. And after the meeting a reporter asked Mom and me some questions, so maybe something will happen from that.

I'm beginning to think Will is right, that I won't be back on the cheer team before the Basswood game. That still makes me sad, but I haven't been thinking about it as much, because I'm getting caught up in this new thing, this fight. Like, I'm thinking I might have to make another video. I'm so mad still about how mean and wrong the superintendent was. I hope I can sleep tonight.

God bless Mom and Will and Uncle Mac. And please, God, help Superintendent Fellows to make better choices. He needs all the help he can get.

twenty

THE NEXT DAY at school, things were about the same. There were some stares and laughter and a mean word or two, but also some secret nods and smiles. It was beginning to feel like a new normal. At lunch, when Joy and Max headed out to the far field after eating their sandwiches, Theresa was hanging out by the climbing bars and angled over to join them. The three girls exchanged easy greetings and started stretching.

After they had been tumbling for a little while, Theresa stopped and pushed her hair out of her eyes, looking back toward the school. "What's he doing?" she said.

Max and Joy looked where she was looking, and

there was Todd, the shy, awkward boy who had told Joy in the hall that he supported her. He was standing a little ways away, watching them. When he saw them looking back, he flinched, turned away, and started walking toward the school.

Max and Joy exchanged a look and a nod of understanding. Then Max jogged toward the retreating boy. When she was close enough, she called out, "Hey, Todd!" Back by the fence, Joy and Theresa watched Max and Todd have a conversation, too quiet for them to hear. "What's she doing?" Theresa asked.

"I think she's asking him if he wants to join us," Joy said. "That's what I'd be doing, and a lot of the time Max and I have the same ideas."

"You want a boy on your squad? He doesn't look like he knows the first thing about cheer."

"The Sparkle Squad is open to everyone." Joy felt a warm feeling in her chest. Now that she had said those words out loud, she realized how right they were.

Todd and Max were walking back together. When all four kids were standing in a little group, Joy said, "Hi."

"Hi," Todd said. "I think it's cool what you're doing. Can I hang out and watch?"

Joy nodded. "I was actually wondering if you wanted to learn how."

Todd blushed and dropped his eyes. "I don't know," he mumbled. "I don't think I should."

Joy and Max exchanged another look. Max said, "Okay, no biggie. Maybe some other time. Stay and watch if you want." So then there were four kids making a Sparkle Squad gathering happen out in the far field. And, this time, it didn't occur to any of them to look to see whether anyone was watching.

When Mom got home that afternoon, she said to Joy, "Remember that reporter we talked to last night? His article posted a little while ago."

"It did? Have you read it? What did he say?"

"I've only skimmed it once, but I think it's pretty good. He wrote what happened. It's reporting."

"Let me see!"

Mother and daughter sat down at the computer together. Mom found the article on the Houston Online website, and they read it together. The headline was TRANS CHEERLEADER BANNED FROM MIDDLE SCHOOL TEAM. Mom was right: the article explained the basic facts of their situation, based on what the reporter had seen for himself in the meeting. "Good, good," Mom said under her breath as they got to the end.

Joy pointed at the screen. "Look, there are comments." There was a button to push to see them, and the counter said there were seven.

Mom said, "Remember, we can't get caught up in this."

"I know, Mom. Click it!"

Mom shook her head a little, but she clicked the button.

The first comment read, *If I caught this kid in the restroom with my kid, I would know what to do,* and then there were two emojis: a gun, and a skull and crossbones.

"Whoa!" Mom shut the laptop.

Joy stared open-mouthed at the closed computer. "They want to shoot me now?"

Mom got up out of her chair and started pacing, which she only did when she was seriously upset, and when Joy reached for the computer, she said sharply, "Don't touch that!" Joy jerked her hand back. Her feelings were at war inside her. Now, for the first time, she felt afraid . . . but another part of her brain was still avidly curious about those other six comments.

Mom, still pacing, had started talking to herself, something else she hardly ever did. "Threats!" she said. "I didn't sign up for threats." Joy could think of nothing to say in response to this. Mom continued to pace and talk. "I wish we had never started this in the first place." She rubbed her face with her hands. "Is it too late to shut everything down? Should we report this? Who would you report it to?"

Joy said tentatively, "Mom?"

"Yes, Joy, what is it?"

"We didn't start it. It was the superintendent who started it."

Mom made a face but said, "Yes, I suppose you're right." Mother and daughter stared at each other for a moment. Then Mom said, "You know what we need right now? We need advice from someone who knows what they're doing. I'm calling Aunt Caroline."

Hey Jojo,

I got a really nasty comment today and Mom was bugging out, but then we called Aunt Caroline and had a long talk on speaker-phone. Aunt Caroline said that it's the inter-net, so people feel like they can say any kind of horrible thing. She also said that it wasn't quite a threat, like, "I am going to find you and kill you." It was more of a show-offy thing, and she said she was almost positive it wasn't real at all. She said she gets comments like that all the time, but the worst thing that has happened is people saying mean things to her in public every once in a while. She also said it's going to happen again, it's part of the fight, but there are things we can do to stay safe, like making sure no one can find out our phone numbers or address. The last thing she said to Mom was, "Jenny, dear, I'm afraid you're already in it. There's no stop-ping now." I don't think Mom liked that much, but she hasn't said anything else about trying to shut it down, so I guess maybe she can see that Aunt Caroline is right. Mom did say she's going to be reading all comments before me from now on, which makes me feel like I'm five, but when I tried to say something, she gave me one of her looks, so I knew she meant it.

There were two other things Aunt Caroline said that were much nicer. One was that everyone at the Rainbow Coalition loves our video. Mom said in a scared voice, "You haven't posted it somewhere, have you?" and Aunt Caroline said, no, of course not, that they would only do that with our permission. But then she said she thought we should make another one and post it, not just in the parent group, but on the big platforms. She said we have a compelling story to tell, and that we could change some minds and do some good for other trans kids in Texas. She also said Uncle Mac could send the footage from the school board meeting for Will to mix into the video, which I thought was an amazing idea. Mom wasn't sure, but I hope she'll say yes, because I'm already thinking of what I want to write and say. Please, God, help Mom see that we don't have a choice now, we just have to keep going . . . keep fighting.

The other nice thing Aunt Caroline said was, "Let's all go out for barbecue on Saturday and talk some more about everything," and Mom said yes right away to that, so we get to see Aunt Caroline again. Yay! I really like her.

God bless Mom and Will and Aunt Caroline and Uncle Mac, and Max and Theresa and Todd, and all our allies. When there are strangers in the world who seem to want to hurt you, it is so good to have allies.

twenty-one

ON THURSDAY JOY could tell Mom was still feeling troubled by the comment on the article, so she tried as hard as she could not to ask about making another video, even though she was itching badly to do it. What the superintendent had said was just so wrong. It needed to be answered.

Mom was thinking about it, though, because she did mention that she had gotten an email from Uncle Mac with a link to download the video from the meeting, and she said, "In case we need it." At that Joy couldn't resist opening her mouth to say something, but she stopped again when Mom held up a warning finger. "Sweetheart, I know you're eager," she said, "but I need more time."

That evening, while Joy was wrestling with

a math worksheet in her room, Max texted. **we talked about you in cheer today.**

Joy picked up and started thumb-typing. **Really?**

rly

How did that happen?

gonna call you

The phone warbled, and Joy tapped to answer. "Hey, goat."

"Hey, rock star. So, it was during circle talk." Circle talk was something that Coach Emily had started. She didn't do it every practice, but if she did, it was usually right at the end, and the idea was they all stood in a circle and held hands, and if anyone had anything on their mind, they could say it, and everyone else would listen.

"What happened?"

"Well, this might surprise you, but it was Theresa who did it. When Coach Emily asked if anyone wanted to talk, she raised her hand, and then she said that she thought it was sad and wrong that you had been kicked off the team."

Joy felt a tingly rush pass through her body. "Wow, that was really nice of her. And brave, too. What happened next?"

"Yeah, this part probably won't surprise you.

Whitney laughed and said, 'That freak?' and some of the other girls laughed too, but then Coach Emily said, 'Girls, remember the honor code—we are to speak respectfully of others at all times,' and Whitney looked super embarrassed."

"Good."

"Then Theresa said, 'I just wanted to mention it, because I think Joy is a really good cheerleader, and the team would be better if she was still on it,' and a bunch of other girls nodded or made sounds like they agreed with her."

"How many of them?" Joy asked eagerly.

Max paused for a second before answering, and Joy wondered if her friend was judging her a little for that question. When she did speak, though, Max's voice was steady. "I don't know exactly, and definitely not everyone, but I'd say a lot."

"Good," Joy said again, also more steadily. "Thank you for telling me."

"You're welcome."

"And, Coach Emily, could you tell . . . how she felt about me being kicked off the team?" This was something Joy had been wondering and worrying about. Did her beloved coach agree with the superintendent's decision?

"I couldn't tell. You know how she is, all official and everything."

"Yeah." When Emily was coaching, she was one hundred percent pure nothing but the coach, and there was no way to know what might be going on inside her head other than that.

Max said, "But it was still a good sign, what she said to Whitney."

"Yeah, it was."

On Friday at lunchtime, out on the far field, Theresa didn't show up at first, so with Todd there they were back down to three, but that didn't last long. The Sparkle Squad saw Theresa coming toward them with not one, but two other girls from the cheer squad, Norah and Becky, who asked if they could hang out and practice too. Joy and Max exchanged an excited look, and then welcomed the new girls warmly. Joy made sure to pull Theresa aside as soon as she could to thank her for speaking up for her in circle time, and Theresa was pleased. "You're welcome," she said, and they smiled at each other.

After stretches and warm-ups, when they were taking turns trying to do a tumbling move called a tick tock, Joy remembered the idea she had had about maybe writing some new cheers. She felt instantly awkward, but also excited to share the idea with the growing squad. Before she lost her nerve, she made herself say right away, "Hey, you guys." Everyone immediately stopped and gave her their full attention, and she blushed, partly from self-consciousness, but also because the attention felt good. She was the leader, she suddenly realized. Or, she and Max were the two leaders, but anyway, she was one. "So, I had an idea the other day. Let's make up some new cheers just for the Sparkle Squad."

There was a chorus of agreement. Joy made herself keep going. "Actually, I've already gotten one kind of started."

"Gucci, let's hear it," Max said.

Joy blushed again and dropped her eyes. "I don't know if it's any good or not," she said. "It's just one line so far."

"Okay, so, tell us what it is, and we can work on it together," Becky said.

Joy looked up again to see open, smiling, expectant faces looking at her. All at once she felt incredibly happy. "You know what?" she said. "You guys are just the absolute best!" On the spur of the moment, she stepped forward and put her hand out, palm down, like they did in practice. Everyone except Todd knew what to do. They all stepped into a tight circle and put their hands on Joy's. Joy glanced at Todd and said, "Come on, you too." Todd looked like he maybe wanted to run away, but he got up from where he usually sat watching and put his hand in as well. Then Joy said, "Sparkle Squad, on three! One, two, three!"

"Sparkle Squad!" everyone shouted, throwing their hands up in the air and dancing back out of the circle. Max did a sparkly thing with her fingers, wiggling them in the air, and the rest copied her, laughing.

After another minute of celebration, Becky said, "So what's this cheer?" and this time Joy felt completely comfortable. "The line I have is, 'Rainbow kids deserve to live,'" she said, and then for the rest of lunch, the Sparkle Squad brainstormed their first original cheer. Everyone had ideas, even Todd, about words or moves or both, and when the bell rang, Joy and Max shared one more high five on the way back in. Something magical had just happened, and they could both see that the other had felt it. The Sparkle Squad was no longer just a little group of friends messing around. It had turned into something more.

Hey Jojo,

Today during lunch, I did a thing with the Sparkle Squad that went really well. I didn't think about it at all. It just felt like the right thing at the right time, and afterward everyone was all excited and working together on a cheer, and we invented a cheer, with a routine and everything. At least, the start of one. I think we can make it better. But the cool thing was, everyone worked on it together. Like a team. We were being a team, and I was being one of the leaders.

The cheer, the way it is now, goes like this:

Rainbow kids deserve to live.

Rainbow kids have so much to give.

Doesn't matter, girl or boy

Rainbow kids should share the joy.

Even if you're in between,

Cheer with me if you know what I mean.

Rainbow kids will always be

Strong and brave and special and free.

Gooooooo, Sparkle Squad!

It's not perfect yet, but the moves that Max and Norah came up with were really good. We'll work on it some more next week, and maybe that will help me feel better about being off the team, because the Basswood game is next Friday, and it's really beginning to look like I won't be back on the team by then.

Tomorrow is barbecue with Aunt Caroline. I can't wait!

God bless everyone on the Sparkle Squad, especially Norah and Becky, who joined today, and Theresa for bringing them. You know what, maybe we need a special thing to do to welcome new members . . . an initiation ceremony. That would be lit. I'll say something about it to Max. And God bless Mom, and Will, and Max in particular, who is the best friend anyone could have, and Aunt Caroline and Uncle Mac, and all the rainbow kids everywhere, who just want to be left alone and who deserve to live, like we said in the cheer.

SPARKLE SQUAD!

twenty-two

THE PLAN FOR dinner was to meet Aunt Caroline at a barbecue truck. Everyone in the Simmons family loved barbecue. It was one of the best gifts Texas had offered when they had moved from the frozen north. They had never been to the truck Aunt Caroline suggested, but Joy liked the looks of it as soon as they pulled into the packed dirt parking lot. It was a bright burnt orange, with red and yellow flames painted around the service window. Several different food trucks were parked around a central area with picnic tables.

Aunt Caroline was already there waiting for them, sitting at a table. She was wearing a crisp skirt and blouse combination, plus tights and low heels, and jewelry and makeup much like the last time, although the colors were different. She had the same enormous purse with her, and she was by far the dressiest person in the whole food court, but it seemed right to Joy. Aunt Caroline obviously cared about looking her best. That was her style.

As they neared the table, Aunt Caroline looked up and called out a greeting, and Joy expressed her approval. "You look really nice," she said, and was surprised when Aunt Caroline's face burst into a big smile.

"Thank you, honey. That means a lot, coming from you."

Joy blushed happily.

Naturally they ordered barbecue all around, though Will chose chicken instead of pork, and of course one of Joy's sides was mac and cheese. While they were waiting for their number to be called, Aunt Caroline said, "So, how has your week been? Mac told me about the school board meeting, and we talked about that nasty post. Any other developments?"

Joy was eager to talk about the Sparkle Squad, but she also still felt a little bit shy with their new friend, so she didn't answer right away. Mom looked thoughtful and said, "It's the nasty post

I've been thinking about most, actually. It really alarmed me."

"That's totally understandable," Aunt Caroline said.

"Thank you for saying that. And yes, it's true, there haven't been any sinister-looking characters lurking on our street or anything. I think you were right, it was just someone saying something outrageous because they could . . . but I can't seem to shake the feeling it gave me."

Aunt Caroline leaned forward, her face serious. "What feeling is that? Can you name it?"

Mom pondered. "It's not exactly fear. There's a yuck factor, that's part of it. Your word 'nasty' is right. It's nasty as in mean, but it's also nasty as in ugly, distasteful. It's gross, that someone would say something like that."

"I hear you."

"And it also makes me feel unsafe."

Aunt Caroline sat back. "Uh-huh. I hear that too." Mom looked as though she was hoping for some words of wisdom. Aunt Caroline tipped her head and made a wry face. "Well, my dears," she said, addressing Joy and Will too, "I guess I would say the bad news is, you are not completely safe.

There is some danger here." Mom frowned. "But the good news is, probably less than you think. In my experience, for every thousand nasty comments, there's only one or two bad experiences, and most of those are not very dangerous either. More in the way of someone getting worked up enough to say something in person. There's a big range between people saying things and people actually doing things, and then even further to go to people doing truly hurtful things."

"I still hate it," Mom said.

"That's totally fair."

There was a silence. Joy was thinking, *But we don't have a choice.* Mom looked at her. "But I have to agree, we don't have a choice," she said. "We're already in it."

Joy said, "I was just thinking that!" and Mom smiled, though her face was still troubled. Joy decided suddenly that now was the time to ask the question she had been holding on to: "So does that mean we can make another video?"

"I'm almost there," Mom said. "There's one more thing that's bothering me."

"What's that?" said Aunt Caroline.

"I went back to the news story to read the

comment again, and to see if there were any more like it, and the comment was gone."

Aunt Caroline said, "That's not surprising. I'm sure the comments are moderated, and once the people at the site realized someone had put something that could be taken as a threat on their platform, they took it down."

Will made eye contact with Joy, and she saw from his face that he wanted to make another video too. He said, "That's good, isn't it? It means someone else saw that it was out of line."

Mom said, "Yes, I suppose that's true. But I took it another way. I thought, if they've taken that nasty comment down, how many more have they also taken down? A few? A dozen? Hundreds?"

Aunt Caroline said, "I've had a lot of experience with things like this, and I feel quite certain that if there were any more comments bad enough to be taken down, it was only one or two." She fiddled with an earring. "It's important to remember that there are more people with us than against us. And of the rest, only a tiny few feel moved to say things like the taken-down comment. But of course we notice and feel every one. They are few but loud. For everyone else, maybe this trans thing is a little weird or worrisome, but they don't really care that much about it."

Their number was called, and for a while everyone was too busy savoring the first bites of delicious barbecue to continue the conversation. Joy was feeling more and more comfortable by the minute, though, and as soon as she had taken off the first edge of her hunger, she told Aunt Caroline about the Sparkle Squad. Aunt Caroline reacted with praise and delight, and Joy soaked it up. "Maybe y'all can cheer at a rally someday," Aunt Caroline said, and Joy filed the idea away. *That would be so cool*, she thought. Part of her mind began working on a question: What would they wear? Her imagination gave her a picture of rainbow pompoms, and she smiled and filed that idea away too.

In the car on the way home, after goodbye hugs with Aunt Caroline, Mom said, "All right, you two, I'm convinced. I may never feel totally safe, but I see we are on a path now, and it's important for us to keep going. You can make another video, and we can pick a platform to post it on."

Will, sitting in the front seat, reached back a hand, and Joy give him a low five.

Hey Jojo,

Will is going to help me shoot another video tomorrow afternoon, and then he's going to put it together with the video that Uncle Mac took at the school board meeting, and we will post it probably Sunday night. I guess this means I'm going to have to watch Uncle Mac's video again, which I really don't want to do, but I have to if I'm going to write the best answer to how wrong the superintendent is getting everything. If you are going to fight, you've got to face your enemy, I guess. I don't like it, but I can do it. I feel strong. Isn't that nice, Jojo? I feel strong. Go me.

God bless Aunt Caroline and Uncle Mac and everyone at the Rainbow Coalition, and Mom and Will, and everyone on the Sparkle Squad and all our allies everywhere. I hope it's true, what Aunt Caroline said, about there being more of us than there are of them. Sometimes I get scared and I start to wonder if there are more of them, but most of the time I feel pretty sure that there are more of us.

twenty-
three

THE NEXT MORNING, after Joy and Mom got home from church, the Simmons family took a deep breath together and then rewatched the video Uncle Mac had shot on his phone at the school board meeting. It was just as unpleasant the second time as it had been when it was happening. Superintendent Fellows looked and sounded like a bully, hard and mean.

Will was as excited as Joy could remember seeing him. Her normally snarky and detached older brother was clearly fascinated by what they were doing together. And, he was good at it. "Let's keep it short," he said intently, "like last time. What we need is the shortest possible clip that shows the worst of what happened at that meeting."

They watched the video again, and when they got to the part where the superintendent talked about indoctrination, Will paused the playback and said, "There. Right there. We can cut in right after he says, 'The issue is,' so his first words are 'The Appleton School District does not support you . . .'"

"That's good," Mom said, and Joy nodded agreement. Mom said, "And where will you cut it off at the other end?"

Will unpaused, and they watched again as Mom in the video said, "That's preposterous," and then tried to explain how the superintendent was getting it wrong, only to be interrupted by him banging his gavel on the table. Will paused again. "Right there," he said. "Look at the expression on his face." In the frozen frame, the camera had caught Mr. Fellows's face in a particularly intense moment, eyes glaring, lips twisted. He looked violent and unhinged. Will said, "I can freeze that image for a second, and then we can cut to Joy's response."

"It's perfect," Joy said. "This is gonna be so cool."

Mom sighed. "I'm still not a hundred percent

happy about this, and I don't think I ever will be. But, my darling daughter, I guess you better start writing."

Joy had been thinking about what to say all week, and the words just flowed. *Mr. Superintendent*, she wrote, *I had to ask my mom what a couple of the words you said mean. She said "indoctrinate" means to force someone to think a certain way, but that's the exact opposite of the truth. Nobody forced me to be the way I am. I just am. Ever since I can remember, I have known in my head and in my heart that I am a girl. If anyone had to change their mind, it was my mom.*

And that other word, "perverted," I just looked it up in the dictionary to be sure, and it looks like it's about stuff my mom says is too adult for me to be thinking about yet. That's horrible. There's nothing naughty or nasty about me. I'm a twelve-year-old girl. I love cheer, and doing art and needlework, and my family, and my dog, and I like hanging out with my friends. Can't you see me, even a little bit? I was sitting right in front of you.

When she finished, she read it aloud to her mother and brother. "Perfect," Mom said, giving her a hug. Then it was time to put on a nice dress, fix her hair, go back into the boy-cave with Will, and shoot. It was easier this time. They both knew what they were doing. When Joy got to the part about head and heart, she tapped her forehead and chest, and when she got to the end, she looked at the camera circle for a second, thinking of the snarling face of the man she was talking to, and added a line she hadn't written. "Mr. Fellows, sir, please, try to open your eyes and see me. I. Am. Just. A. Girl."

She stared another second at the camera, and then Will said "And . . . cut!"

"Cut?" Joy said. "You sound like you're making a movie."

Will looked bashful. "I really like doing this a lot," he said. "So maybe someday I'll actually make a movie!"

"Gucci," Joy said. "I hope you do, Will. And thank you. Do you think our video's good? Should we do a retake?"

"I think it's great. You nailed it."

By Sunday evening the video was ready to post. Will had put the two pieces together, so that it was super clear that Joy was answering the superintendent. He had also added some text. At the beginning, on a black screen, it said *Apple-ton, Texas, school board meeting*, with the date. When the superintendent came on screen, words appeared saying who he was. When Uncle Mac's camera shifted to Mom saying, "That's preposterous," the words *Jennifer Simmons* appeared. And when it was Joy's turn, she got words too: *Twelve-year-old trans activist Joy Simmons.*

"Can we say that?" Joy said. "Am I an activist now?"

Will looked at Mom, who said, "You sure are, honey. You're putting yourself right out there."

While Will had been doing his production work, there had been an email exchange with Aunt Caroline, making a plan. They would post the video at a certain time on the social media platform they had chosen, and then the Rainbow Coalition, which had thousands of followers, would repost it immediately, and then they would see what happened after that.

Joy had a jumpy stomach, but not as much as the first time. Mom had made a couple of rules: they could watch for one hour, with Mom checking the comments first, from the posting time of eight p.m. to nine p.m., and then whatever was happening, no computers until morning. Joy complained about that, but secretly she was relieved. She was beginning to see how it was important to have time away from the internet.

Eight o'clock came. Mom hovered her finger, said, "Okay, ready or not, here we go," and clicked post. All three members of the Simmons family leaned forward to see what would happen.

It was a lot like the first time, just bigger and faster. In the hour that they watched, instead of dozens of views and likes and reposts and comments, they got a few hundred, but otherwise in the comments it was the same even mix between positive and negative, understanding and wrong, lots of allies and a few trolls. There was plenty of scornful or sarcastic or insulting language, but nothing like the gun-and-skull comment that had been on the news site. So when Mom said gently, "Nine o'clock, time to shut it down," Joy didn't even pretend to put up a fight. She felt a powerful urge to lie in bed for a little while before sleeping and read a real book. She couldn't remember the last time she had felt so tired of looking at screens and thinking about what they showed her.

Hey Jojo,

My second video is out in the world, and there are a whole bunch of total strangers watching it right now, and some of them are thinking nice things about me, and some of them are thinking mean or scared or stupid or wrong things about me, and I guess it's good that we did it, but right now I am glad none of those people know where I live, and that none of them know who I really am. I'm glad I'm alone in my room, with Will in his room next door, and Mom in the living room reading, and the doors locked for the night.

I wonder what school will be like tomorrow. Will anyone see the video? Mom said they might not, because last time, even though we got fewer views and stuff, it was in the parents' forum. This time a lot more people are watching, but they are all over the country. The world, even. So maybe not. I hope not. But whatever happens, I'll deal with it.

God bless Mom and Will, who is maybe going to make movies someday, which is so cool, and God bless Aunt Caroline and Uncle Mac and the Sparkle Squad, and God bless this home, and the real world, and all the good people in it who are allies or at least cool with just leaving me and kids like me alone so we can live our lives in peace.

twenty-four

ENTERING SCHOOL ON Monday morning, Joy was once again on high alert, watching for new reactions, but there didn't seem to be any. Mom had been right about the difference between the community forum and the wide-open field of posting on social media. They were getting more attention than before, but none of it seemed to be local.

Over the next few days, the feeling of a new, slightly more complicated normal continued. There were mocking looks, mean laughs, and a few insults to be dealt with, mostly by ignoring them; and on the other side, there were more subtle or outright statements of support. One of these was from Devon, one of maybe two kids at school who openly said they were gay. Joy and Devon had language arts class together, and when the bell rang at the end of class on Tuesday, he came over.

"Hey, Joy," he said.

"Hey, Devon."

"Could I just tell you, I think it's a shame that the school kicked you off the cheer team."

"Thank you, I appreciate it." Devon nodded and turned to go, and Joy said, "Hey, you want to hang out with us at lunch? We have this thing called the Sparkle Squad going, and it's kinda about cheer, but it's also just about being together."

"Sure. Sounds like fun."

"Gucci. See you at lunch."

Another new person also showed up that day, a girl named Rachel, who had a goth emo style and mostly kept to herself. She came with Todd, who awkwardly introduced her as his friend and asked if she could hang out. "Of course," Joy and Max said together, and the Sparkle Squad had grown by two new members.

By Wednesday, Joy's new video had gotten several hundred more views and likes, and dozens more comments and reposts, and then the internet found something new to pay attention to, and the numbers stopped changing much. There were plenty of icky posts, but nothing outright scary. That afternoon, when Mom got home from work, she said, "Sweetheart, I have a surprise for you."

"Yes? What is it? Are you finally going to buy me a sewing machine?" Joy had been begging for a real sewing machine since she was five, even though she knew the answer was always going to be *not yet*, or *I'm sorry, honey, we can't afford that right now* or both.

"No, I'm still working on that one. This is different. You know people can message me through the platform we posted the video on? Well, today I got a message from someone we've heard of."

"Who, who?"

"It's a message from Kimberly Shappley." Joy looked blank, so Mom said, "Kai's mom."

"What? No! That's so amazing! What did she say?"

"She said we did a nice job on the video, and she offered to have a video call with us if we want, to talk about trans activism in Texas."

"They want to talk to us?"

"So it seems."

"Do you think we should?" Joy felt instantly nervous about the possibility of talking to Kai.

After all, she had videos with millions of views.

"Sweetheart, I already answered and set it up. We're talking with them at seven, after dinner."

Then there was more jumpy-stomach time to get through. Dinner was tacos, one of Joy's favorites, so that helped. By 6:55 p.m. she was sitting in front of the computer, jittering with excitement. She had changed her mind twice about what to wear, settling finally on her Appleton East cheer shirt, and she had asked her mother to help her do her hair.

As Mom sat down she said, "Breathe, honey. I'm sure they're regular folks just like us."

When Kai and her mother appeared on the laptop screen, they were sitting close together with a bulletin board behind them that had stickers and flags and pictures on it. It was hard to see details, but it looked like it all had to do with Kai's activism. Kai looked older than in her testimony video, but she was the same pretty, bright-eyed, blond-haired girl. The moms did hellos and introductions, and then Kai waved and smiled a warm smile and said, "Hi, I'm Kai!"

Joy pushed through a rush of nerves and managed to say, "Hi, I'm Joy. It's an honor to meet you."

Kai tossed her hair over her shoulder and

struck a pose like a queen. "Why, *thenk* you," she said grandly. "I am quite fabulous, I know." For one second Joy was awed—and then she realized it was all a put-on, and the two girls laughed together. In her regular voice, Kai said, "It's nice to meet you, too. I liked your video."

"I was inspired by you," Joy said. "I saw the video of you testifying about that bill, and I thought, 'Wow, she's so good. Maybe someday I could be as good as that.'"

Kai smiled, clearly pleased. "Awesome—that means a lot!"

Kimberly was nodding. "That's really encouraging to hear," she said, "because we need as many voices as we can get in this fight right now. It's getting bad here in Texas."

Then for a while it was two moms talking to each other. Kimberly explained about bills that some lawmakers were trying to pass that were awful for trans kids and their families. There was one in particular, she said, that scared her. The idea of it was to make it legal for the state to take trans kids away from their parents. Kimberly said that next week there was going to be a hearing in a committee to talk about the bill, and that if they wanted to, the Simmonses could come to Austin and join the Shappleys in testifying against it. Joy's heart leapt at the idea of testifying like Kai, but she was not surprised when Mom said, "We'll think about it."

Next the moms talked about safety. Kimberly said the Shappley family had a plan for if someone showed up at their house looking to cause trouble. She also said that she monitored all of Kai's social media accounts, and Joy did not like the look her mother gave her. She valued her freedom. She hadn't mentioned to her mother that a few nasty comments had started showing up in her feeds. Kai's mom also said, "I tell Kai all the time, it's my job to worry, and it's her job to be a kid," and Mom nodded with a thoughtful expression on her face.

Kai looked like she was getting a little bored, and Joy thought, *I wonder how many calls like this they've done.* When the moms came to a pause, Kai sat up suddenly and said, "Hey, Joy, you wanna meet my cat?" and when Joy said she would love to, Kai dove out of the frame to fetch the cat, and then they were talking pets, and Joy thought, *I like this girl a lot. I wonder if maybe we could be friends.*

Hey Jojo,

I think Mom liked Kai's mom, because almost right away they started talking like they were old friends. I've noticed that Mom can be sort of shy and quiet when she doesn't like someone, but she was just chatting away.

Mom said "we'll see" about going to Austin to testify, but I think she must be changing her mind about how brave to be in this new world, because right after the call, without me asking, she asked if I wanted to go. Of course I said yes, yes, yes! And now I will get to meet Kai in person!

God bless Mom and Will, and the Sparkle Squad, and Kai and Kimberly Shappley. They seem like great people, and it was amazing to meet them.

twenty-five

OVER THE NEXT week, Mom and Kimberly Shappley had a long conversation by text and email. It was decided that Mom and Joy would go to Austin so that Joy could testify against the bill, which, if it became a law, would allow the state of Texas to take Joy away from her mother. She would not be testifying in front of the whole senate, like Kai had done in her viral video when it had been her mother's job that was threatened. Instead, she would be testifying in front of a committee that was taking a first look at the bill. That was fine with Joy. She was nervous enough as it was.

Kimberly told Mom what to expect, including that they might have to wait a long time to get their turn to speak, so it was going to be a daylong affair. Kimberly also warned them that there might be some people there who would tell terrible lies about trans kids, but then she added that there was also a group of parents and kids and allies who showed up over and over again for things like this. **We've gotten to be like family,** Kimberly said in one of her texts. **I look forward to introducing you to them.**

"Won't that be nice," Mom said. "You'll get to meet more kids like you."

"Yes, it'll be nice," Joy said, and she meant it, even though what she was looking forward to most of all was meeting Kai face-to-face. The mothers had given permission for the two girls to connect through a messaging app, and they were getting to know each other. Kai was funny, and intense about her chickens, and Joy liked her more and more. She didn't say so in any texts, because she didn't feel sure how Kai might take it, but she was starting to feel like she had found a sister, and it was an amazing feeling.

At school, the Sparkle Squad had evened out at about ten people a day, with some kids showing up every day and others just some days. It was still a mix of kids from the cheer team, plus Todd and

Rachel and a few more of the other kids who didn't quite fit in and lurked around the edges of things.

Joy still saw Whitney in the halls every day, and Whitney never passed on the chance to whisper a comment or laugh or both, but Joy was getting better at ignoring her.

On Wednesday, the day before the day off to go to Austin, Joy had an unexpected encounter. It was with Carmen, the haughty cheerleader whose mother had complained about Joy, and who kept giving Joy looks. At first Joy had assumed that the looks were scornful, but over time she felt less sure. So it was not a total surprise when Carmen found her in the cafeteria at lunchtime and said, "Hey, Joy."

Joy turned, saw who was speaking, and braced herself. "Hey," she said warily. "What's up?"

Carmen looked around. No one seemed to be paying attention. She blushed a little, leaned close, and said in a near whisper, "I've heard about your Sparkle Squad, and I think it's great what you're doing."

"Wow, thank you. That's nice of you, considering—"

Carmen blushed harder and dropped her eyes.

"Yeah, my mom. I just want you to know, I didn't ask her to do that."

"You didn't?"

"No. Honestly, I don't care if you are trans, but she does, and I didn't know how to stop her. Just . . . sorry about my mom."

"Thanks," Joy said. The idea of inviting Carmen to join the Sparkle Squad popped into her head, but the other girl was already turning away.

The conversation with Carmen helped Joy feel more confident about testifying the next day, which was good, because Mom had a couple of pieces of bad news when she got home. The first was that Kimberly had messaged her to say that Kai's little brother Kaleb had come down with a fever, so the Shappleys would not be at the State House in the morning. "I'm afraid you're not going to meet your new friend after all, at least not this time," Mom said.

"You mean I'm going to have to testify alone?" Joy had been counting on Kai to go first and show her how.

"Not alone, sweetheart. Remember Kimberly said lots of other families will be there." That was true, but Joy still felt rattled, as well as disappointed that she wouldn't be meeting her new fabulous friend.

The other piece of news Mom had was that online reaction to the second video had suddenly picked up again. She had an expression on her face when she said it that Joy recognized—it was the face she made when she was about to say something she knew her kids wouldn't like. Joy's mood dropped another notch. Mom said, choosing her words carefully, "Apparently what happened was, someone with a podcast found the video and decided to talk about it." Joy smiled and raised her eyebrows, and Mom said, "No, it's not a good thing. At least not this time. This particular podcaster is rigid and extreme in his views, and he likes to say mean things, to attack people, and this time he picked you to attack."

"Can we listen?" Joy said.

"No, sweetheart, I'm afraid not," Mom said. "I'm remembering what Kimberly said, about how it's my job to worry and your job to be a kid. I know you value your freedom online, but this time I'm setting a limit. I listened a little, just enough to get an idea, and it was hateful and horrible, and you don't need to hear it."

Joy stared at her mother. Her feelings were all mixed up inside. She knew she ought to be angry and fight back to protect her freedom, but on the other hand, Mom looked really upset. So, instead of trying to think of a way to argue, Joy said, "Was it really that bad?"

Mom nodded. "It was really bad, honey," she said gently. "The comments too. This time there weren't any allies to balance all the hate and meanness. You don't need to be exposed to that."

"Got it, Mom," Joy said meekly, and her mother smiled sadly and gave her a long hug.

"We're going to be fine," Mom said. "It's scary, but I'm beginning to believe that it's like everyone has told us. There is a little risk, but the danger is not usually real."

Hey Jojo,

Tomorrow I'm getting off school to go to Austin to testify. I've written my testimony, just like getting ready for a video. Mom is going to try to video me on her phone, but if it doesn't come out right, Will says we can record it again in his room, just like the other times. So now I'm not just talking to the superintendent, I'm talking to the people who run our state. I'm pretty nervous, but Will said something that helped me. He said, "You already know how to do this. Just pretend you're talking to the camera, but then look at people's faces every once in a while, so they know you're talking straight to them."

Will is a pretty good brother. Who knew?

Mom made some new rules tonight about going online. She said I could still message with my friends, but not go on my social media except when she's there. I'm pretty okay with the new rules. There was something about her face when she told me about the podcast. She looked scared. But then she said we're still going to testify. A little risk, she said. I can live with a little risk, I think.

God bless Mom and Will, and the Sparkle Squad, and Aunt Caroline and Uncle Mac, who we just found out is driving us to Austin tomorrow, and Carmen for telling me she doesn't agree with her mom.

twenty-six

IN THE CAR on the way to Austin in the morning, Uncle Mac sang along with the radio and told funny stories and got Mom and Joy laughing, so that Joy almost forgot to be nervous. Joy couldn't remember the last time she had met a person who seemed as happy as Uncle Mac, and the three hours on the highway slipped quickly by.

The Texas Capitol turned out to be a big, impressive building made of stone. It sat up on a rise with wide green parks, surrounded by a spiky fence, and it had a huge dome with a statue on top and flags flying on either side. Uncle Mac said some people called it the Big Pink Dome, because over time the rock that the building was made of had turned a little bit pink. Joy liked that. They had to go through security to get in, and inside it was like an enormous maze. Everything was big and made of more stone, floors and walls and high ceilings, with long halls stretching almost out of sight, columns everywhere, and dozens and dozens of big, heavy wooden doors.

Uncle Mac led them to one of the doors, in a hall down in what felt like the basement, where at least the ceilings were a little bit lower. He had warned them that they would be arriving while the committee meeting was in session, and that it would be important to be quiet. The plan was to slip in at the back and sit down. It was impossible to carry out that plan, though, because the room was completely full. Peeking through the little window in the door, they saw every seat filled and people standing crowded at the back. Other people were standing around in the hall, clearly waiting to get in.

"I thought this might happen," Uncle Mac whispered. "We have a bunch of people here to testify, and I'm afraid the other side does too. Although a lot of these folks could be here for other bills too. But it's okay. Wait here, and I'll see about signing you up to speak." Then he squeezed inside the door, and Joy watched him through the window as he filled out a little pink card at a table just inside the door and handed it to an official-looking person. He squeezed back out and whispered, "You're signed up. Now we just have to wait."

They found a place along the wall to stand, and Joy looked curiously at the people around them. There were several other kids there, and Joy wondered if they were trans. The committee they were there to talk to made all the laws about how children were treated by the state, so they might be there for other reasons. She smiled shyly at some of the kids, and a few smiled back.

There were also a couple of people out in the hall who seemed like they might be part of what Uncle Mac called the other side. There was one woman who kept staring at Joy. The woman had a hard, angry-looking face. Uncle Mac stared back, then took a step toward the woman. "Do we have a problem?" he said. The woman scowled and turned away. Uncle Mac leaned down and said quietly to Joy, "Yeah, some of them have hate in their hearts. But don't worry, nothing bad can happen here."

Presently two families showed up who were clearly there about the trans bill, because they had signs. *Proud parent of a trans child*, said one. The other said, *No on HB 1204*, which was the number of the bill, and underneath it said, *Leave my kid alone*. Each family had one or two parents, and one child.

Joy glanced up at Mom with a question in her eyes. Mom said, "Do you want to say hello?" Joy nodded. They went over, and Mom started a conversation. It was a little awkward at first, because of how strange and grand their surroundings were, but then Mom mentioned the Shappleys, and the other parents knew them. Then Joy was meeting the two other kids, a girl named Linda and a boy name Toby, who were trans just like her. The kids were friendly, and a few minutes after that, the parents were having to hush their children because they were forgetting to keep quiet as they played around in the hall.

Uncle Mac and Aunt Caroline had been right—it was a long wait. Finally, there was a break, and a bunch of people left, so they could go in and sit down. Once they were inside, Joy examined the room. It had wood panel walls, a couple of paintings of old white men, and ranks of chairs facing the front, where long tables were set up in a U shape. The committee sat in big high-backed chairs behind the tables. There were eleven committee members, eight men and three women, and they were well-dressed and mostly looked old enough to be grandparents. Each of them had a name plate and a microphone in front of them, and they all looked quite serious and professional. Joy started to feel nervous again.

Toby and his mom had sat down next to them, and Toby noticed her looking. He pointed to one woman whose name plate read *Sen. Hawthorn* and said, "I met her once. She's an ally."

Uncle Mac heard and said, "That's right. It's important to remember, not everyone on the committee is against us."

"Really?" Joy said.

Uncle Mac nodded. He did a quick scan of the people behind the long tables and said, "At least four of them are definitely on our side, and a couple more might be undecided."

"How do you know?" Joy whispered.

"Oh, we keep track. It's important to know who your lawmakers are."

Joy sat back, feeling a little better. It helped to know there were friends in the room.

Presently the chairman, a man with silver hair who sat in a chair with a higher back in the middle of the middle table, tapped his gavel and said, "I'm opening the hearing on HB 1204."

twenty-seven

UNCLE MAC, SITTING next to Mom, whispered to them what was happening. "First," he said, "the senator who sponsored the bill will introduce it."

"What does that mean, to sponsor?" Joy whispered back.

"It means it was his idea. He's the one who wants it to be a law. So this might be pretty unpleasant. I'm sorry you have to hear this."

An old man in a suit had gotten up from a chair in the front row of the audience. He sat down at a little table that faced the committee and started talking into the microphone that was there. Joy was braced for any sort of nastiness, but it didn't seem like that at all, at least at first. The man had a mumbly way of talking, and his sentences seemed to go on forever, so Joy had trouble understanding what he was saying. It was something about protecting children, and that seemed good . . . but then Joy began to understand that he meant protecting children from their parents forcing them to be trans. He didn't say "indoctrinate," but it was the same idea in other words, and it was just as completely wrong and insulting an idea as before. Joy shifted in her seat, and Mom put her hand on her leg and said under her breath, "Patience, sweetie. I know, it's horrible. But it's his turn now. We'll get ours in a little bit."

When the senator was done talking, he got up and walked slowly out, leaning on a cane. Joy tried to catch his eye, but he looked straight ahead. It seemed he didn't want to see any of the kids in the room. Then the chairman picked up the stack of pink cards that was in front of him and called a name, and the testimony began.

Now that her name could be called at any time, Joy's nerves began to jangle. She double-checked her phone, where she had the testimony ready to read. It was still there. She did her best to breathe and keep her legs from jittering, and to pay attention. She also started keeping score on her fingers, counting how many were for the bill and so against trans kids, and how many were against the bill and so for trans kids. That led to a pleasant surprise—almost everyone was there to testify against the bill.

There was a doctor who treated trans kids. She talked about how such treatment was safe, normal, and necessary. "All the major medical associations agree that this is good treatment and that it saves lives," she said.

There were a couple of activists who spoke, including someone from the Lone Star Rainbow Coalition. "If you pass this law, you are bullying our kids, plain and simple," one said. There were parents of trans kids, who said things like, "If this bill becomes law, we are going to have to move out of Texas."

There were still a few on the other side, though. One was the fierce-eyed lady from out in the hall, who started out loud and got louder, practically shouting at the committee. What she was saying didn't make much sense to Joy. The woman mentioned Satan, Judgment Day, devil spawn, and sin. The members of the committee sat still and watched her, just as they had with all the other speakers, giving no sign of what they thought. At last, the shouting woman finished and left, and then the chairman looked at the next card and said clearly, "Joy Simmons."

Joy felt her mind go instantly blank. She clutched her phone and stood up. She glanced to her right and saw Uncle Mac giving her an encouraging smile and a thumbs-up. Mom squeezed her shoulder. Then Joy made her way up to the front of the room and sat down at the table.

The chairman said politely, "Welcome, Joy. Go ahead whenever you are ready."

Joy felt frozen. She was shaking. She squeezed her eyes shut and took a shuddery breath. *Come on, Joy*, she thought fiercely to herself. *You can do this. Remember who is with you.* She thought of Mom and Uncle Mac watching her from their seats. She thought of Will saying, *Take your time.* She thought of Max and the Sparkle Squad. She thought of her brand-new friends right here in the room, Toby and Linda.

Then she thought of Kai, remembering how calm her hero had been, talking to more people in a bigger room. "Be like Kai," she whispered to herself. Then she took another deep breath, easier this time, opened her eyes, brought her text up on her phone, and began to read.

"Hello. My name is Joy Simmons, and I am twelve years old. I live with my mom and my brother, Will, in Appleton, Texas. I am in the seventh grade at Appleton East Middle School, and I am a transgender girl." Joy stopped to look up at the committee. She saw the same still faces as before, except for the one woman Toby had said was an ally, Senator Hawthorn, who smiled a little and nodded. That helped her to go on.

"I love cheer, and I also like art and needlework and reading and texting with my friends." The next line on her screen was about the bill, but she didn't feel like she was quite done with the first part yet, so she added a line: "So, as you can see, I'm just a regular kid." Going off script felt scary, so she gripped her phone tighter and went back to reading.

"I am here today because I learned recently that some lawmakers want to make it so the state can take me away from my mom because she takes care of me. I can't understand why anyone would want to make a law like that. My mom is an amazing mom who takes good care of me. When I told her that I was a girl, she could see that it was true. She believed me, and she helped me be my real self in the world." To her alarm, Joy suddenly felt like she was about to cry, but she forced herself to keep going, even though her throat felt squeezy and tears were pressing behind her eyes.

"My mom loves me, and I love her. We are a family. The idea that you would take me away is mean and bad and wrong." She wiped at the corner of her eye. "So please, do the right thing and say no to this horrible law. Please leave me alone and let me live my life and grow up in peace, at home with my family where I belong." She looked up again. Senator Hawthorn was smiling and her eyes were shining, and a couple of the other senators looked like they were paying more attention, too, although Joy couldn't guess what they were thinking. "So, that's it," she finished, suddenly feeling terribly self-conscious. "Thank you for listening to my testimony."

To Joy's surprise, people in the room started to clap. The chairman banged his gavel. "Order," he said sharply. In a gentler voice he said, "Thank you, Joy." Then he called a new name.

Joy returned to her seat, shaking now with

relief. She felt hot and cold both at once, and her ears were buzzing. Mom gave her a big squeeze and whispered, "Well done, sweetheart. I am so proud of you." Uncle Mac was grinning from ear to ear and gave her a double thumbs-up. Toby high-fived her. It took her heartbeat and breathing a couple of minutes to return to normal.

Hey Jojo,

It was so scary testifying today, but I guess I did fine. Everyone said so, anyway. In the car on the way home, Uncle Mac said I was a natural. That was nice to hear. And Mom said three times that she was proud of me.

I made two new friends, and one of them, Linda, testified too, and I thought she did a good job. My other new friend, Toby, didn't testify, but his mom did, and she was good too.

Everyone on our side was good, saying real things from their hearts. The few people on the other side either seemed a little bit nuts, like this one lady who talked about Satan, or they were just lost in completely wrong ideas about us. Why do people have such wrong ideas about us? I wish I understood that.

God bless Mom and Will, and Uncle Mac, and Max and the whole Sparkle Squad and my new friends Toby and Linda, who I think we'll get to meet again, because Mom traded phone numbers with their parents, and God bless Kai and her mom and brother, who I hope is feeling better, and her cats, her chickens, and her favorite person in the whole world: Dolly Parton. I still hope I'll get to meet Kai someday. Thinking of her helped me talk today, and I want to thank her.

twenty-eight

LITTLE BY LITTLE, the Simmons family's lives had gotten as busy as they had been when Joy had been on the cheer team. A day was coming in early November when two important things were going to happen both on the same day, and both of them were going to take some work to get ready for. Talking about it, Mom and Joy started calling it the Big Day.

The first thing that was going to happen on the Big Day was, the people fighting against HB 1204 were going to rally in Austin, because on that day the committee was meeting again to decide what to do about the bill. Uncle Mac explained that they could send it on to the full senate with a recommendation that it pass, or a recommendation that it not pass; or there were ways they could decide not to send it at all, which was called "killing the bill."

The activists were hoping for anything but the first choice, so they were planning to gather outside one of the entrances to the Capitol, where most of the senators went in to start their day's work. They would hold signs and sing and give speeches and do whatever they could to make sure the senators would know that HB 1204 was a terrible bill, and that it was the lives of real kids that they would be destroying if they passed it.

Joy was excited about going to the rally, because the Shappleys were planning to be there. Then she got even more excited about going, because, in their ongoing text conversation, Kai had a wonderful idea. Of course, one of the things they were chatting about was cheer—Kai liked cheer too, although she had never been on a team—and when Joy told Kai about the Sparkle Squad, and especially about the "Rainbow Kids" cheer they had now perfected, Kai said, **You know what would be amazing? If the Sparkle Squad could come to the rally and do that cheer.**

Joy instantly remembered that Aunt Caroline

had suggested cheering at a rally too. Her mind began to race. She would need to ask Mom, and there would need to be fabulous costumes, and rainbow pompoms if they could be found in time. After thanking Kai effusively, Joy signed off and went looking for her mother. By sheer luck, she found Mom in video conversation with Aunt Caroline and reminded them about the idea.

Aunt Caroline was thrilled and said that a squad of rainbow kids doing a cheer would be the highlight of the rally. Mom, predictably, hemmed and hawed a little bit about how complicated it would be to get a bunch of kids out of school on a Tuesday and up to Austin for the day, but before the video call was over, Joy was given permission to mention the idea to the other members of the squad. Even if a few of them could come, Joy thought, it could still be incredibly awesome.

When she mentioned the idea to the squad the next day at lunch, she got a mixed reaction. Max immediately thought it was an amazing idea, if her parents said she could go. Max's instant excitement helped a couple of the other kids who were on the school cheer team say at least halfway enthusiastic things, but Joy could tell that their hearts weren't completely in it. To Joy's surprise, after Max it was the non-cheer-team kids who were most willing—Todd and Rachel and Devon. "It's a chance for us to stand up for ourselves," Devon said, and the other two nodded in agreement. "And for you, Joy."

"You'd have to learn at least some basic moves," Joy said. "If we're going, I really think we should all cheer." The three kids looked at each other, then nodded. Joy made a mental note that whatever costume idea they came up with, it would need to have an option for kids who dressed more masc.

The other thing that was happening on the Big Day was the next meeting of the school board. By now Mom was in almost daily contact with either Aunt Caroline or Uncle Mac, and everyone agreed that it was worth going back and trying to confront the superintendent again.

By itself, going to another meeting was maybe not that complicated, but this meeting would not be as simple as the last one, because the extra attention from the nasty podcast had started the debate in the parents' group again, and it had quickly gotten much bigger and uglier than it had been before. Mom wouldn't let Joy look, which made Joy feel frustrated, but Mom just shook her head and said, "Remember Kimberly's rule. My job is to worry. Your job is to be a kid."

Mom did say that the posts in the parents' group weren't so much about Joy anymore. People were arguing in a general way, she said, about whether trans was real or not, and whether parents who supported their trans kids were hurting their kids or not. "There's a lot of completely wrong information, and a lot of strong feelings," she said. "And people on both sides are talking about showing up at the next meeting of the school board, so it won't be just us this time." A plan was made for both Aunt Caroline and Uncle Mac to come to the meeting with them, just in case things got out of hand.

A couple of nights before the Big Day, they had another dinner out with Aunt Caroline—authentic local Mexican food this time—and Joy got to ask her for more of her story. Aunt Caroline said, "When I was growing up, it wasn't like it is now. Now if you want information about what it means to be trans, or if you want examples of trans people, you can find all of that online. When I was a kid, there was nothing. Like you, I always knew I was a female person on the inside, but I had no words, no information, no examples I could point to. I was also a dutiful, obedient kid, so by the time I was five or six I had already decided that the only choice I had was to be the best possible boy and man I could be, even though it felt completely fake and wrong, because that was what everyone expected. So I playacted manhood until I was in my forties, and it was pretty awful, like I was slowly dying inside. But then finally I couldn't take it any longer, and I came out and transitioned."

Mom said gently, "That must have been hard."

"It was. I lost a spouse and a job, and most of my family won't talk to me anymore. But it was absolutely essential. I had gotten to the point where if I couldn't live my authentic life, I was going to self-destruct. The hardest part, though, is the years I lost. I could have been a girl on the outside too, from the beginning, like you. I could have been a young woman in the world. But I didn't know how, and I lost those years, and I'll never get them back."

There was a somber silence. The question Joy had asked herself after testifying came back into her head. "Aunt Caroline, why do people have such wrong ideas about us?"

"That's an excellent question. The best answer I have come up with is, there are a lot of people who feel unsafe or left out or left behind or all three, and when folks feel like that, they can sometimes feel a lot more comfortable if someone tells them a story in which the unsafe-feeling people are the Good Guys, and someone else is the Bad Guy. I guess people need someone to blame, or to fight against. And then other people, politicians and TV people and people online who are cynical and mean, make up awful stories about people like us. They pick us to be their Bad Guys, so they can sell things to the unsafe-feeling people and control them."

Hey Jojo,

The day after tomorrow, five of us on the Sparkle Squad are going to Austin to cheer at a rally and try to get the committee to kill that awful bill. We're going to have costumes and rainbow pompoms! It turns out Max's mom likes to sew, so she's doing the costumes, which is just matching shirts for everyone and a choice between skirts and shorts, and Mom found sparkly rainbow ribbons at a party store to make the pompoms out of, so we're going to look good. And then after the rally we're driving back home to go to another school board meeting. It's going to be a wild day, and I'm afraid it might have people being nasty in it, but it will also have many friends and allies.

God bless Mom and Will, and Aunt Caroline and Uncle Mac, and all the Sparkle Squad, whether they can come to the rally or not, and Kai and her mom, and all the friends and allies.

twenty-nine

WHEN THE BIG Day came, it was a three-car caravan to get Joy, Mom, Will, Uncle Mac, four more members of the Sparkle Squad—Max, Todd, Rachel, and Norah—and several parent chaperones to Austin. They had to leave very early, and Joy had not gotten much sleep the night before, so she dozed a little in the car while Uncle Mac and Mom chatted and sang along with the radio. Joy was surprised that Will said he wanted to join, but she was not surprised that he had put in his earbuds and disappeared into his phone.

Once they had found parking as close to the Capitol as they could, they headed to the door where the protesters had agreed to gather. As they approached, they saw a group of people with signs, and Joy began eagerly scanning the crowd for Kai's long blond hair. It didn't take long to find her. The two girls caught each other's eyes, and Kai broke away from her mother's side and came running over. Before she felt quite ready, Joy was standing face-to-face with her idol. Feeling suddenly awkward and shy, she held out her hand to shake. "Hi, I'm Joy," she said formally.

Kai gave the hand a look and said, "How about a hug instead?" Joy nodded fervently, and then Kai stepped forward and wrapped her arms around Joy's neck in an exuberant hug. "Joy!" Kai exclaimed. "It's so awesome to finally meet you in person!"

After a second, Joy hugged back, and she felt something loosen inside her. Kai might have millions of views, and she had an electric star presence when you met her in person, but she was also open and kind, and they were already friends. When they broke out of the hug, they were both grinning. "I am so glad to meet you too," Joy gushed.

Joy's family, Uncle Mac, and the Sparkle Squad had all been watching, and Kai now turned to them. "Hi, y'all!" she said brightly, waving a hand, even though they were all right there. There was a chorus of hellos in return. Kai zeroed in on the Sparkle Squad, already wearing their costumes. "And you must be the Sparkle Squad!" she said. The members of the squad nodded and agreed. "It's fabulous that y'all are here," Kai said. "I can't wait to hear y'all's cheer."

In the last few seconds, Kimberly Shappley had walked over to join them. Joy, looking at her face in person for the first time, thought, *She looks friendly and smart and strong, all at once.* "Hi, y'all," Kai's mom said when she reached them. "Welcome to Austin. I see you've already met my little force of nature."

"Mom!" Kai said in mock outrage.

"Drama queen, then," said Kimberly.

"The most magnificent in the world," Kai said, with a toss of her head. Everyone chuckled, and then the grown-ups were introducing themselves, and Kai turned again to Joy. "Let me show you the setup," she said, and just like that they were talking as easily as if they had been friends since they were three.

The arrangement was simple. So far about forty people were present, with more trickling in. The door next to where they were staging their rally had a broad paved place in front of it, and those who had brought signs were standing in two short lines, one on either side, so that lawmakers going in had to walk between them. The signs had messages on them like *I love my trans kid* and *No on HB 1204* and *Stop bullying my child*. There were also trans flags and rainbow flags. It looked like there were several families there, with maybe a dozen kids running around. Halfway along one of the two lines there was also a podium with a microphone set up and the Lone Star Rainbow Coalition—a star with rainbow colors inside it—on the front.

"We're early still," Kai said. "The senators usually arrive in the last fifteen minutes or so before the meeting is supposed to start, so that's when we'll have a couple of speeches, and y'all can do your cheer."

"Are you giving a speech?" Joy asked.

"Not this time. It's my mom's turn."

For the next little while Joy stood at the end of one of the lines, holding a light pink, blue, and white trans flag that a nice stranger loaned to her. After a few minutes, she saw another face she knew—Toby, from the hearing. The two families greeted each other warmly and stood together. As the hour of the meeting approached, a couple of people with cameras showed up, one a camera for taking still photos, and another an actual video camera, for TV. Senators started showing up too. They were easy to pick out, because of their formal clothes and name tags. Most of them kept their eyes down and ignored the protestors. A few smiled and nodded. It was time to start.

Kimberly was the first speaker. As she began, the man with the video camera filmed her. She spoke without notes, easily and naturally. "Y'all," she said, "there was a time in my life when I would have supported this bill. I grew up in rural Mississippi, and I used to be a preacher in one of the megachurches over in Houston, and I believed as I had been taught. Back in those days, I would have seen families like ours as lost in sin, in the clutches of Satan." A murmur passed through the crowd. "But then Kai came into my life, and she knew who she was from day one. When she was as young as eighteen months old she was telling me every way she could that she was a girl. I resisted at first, tried to fight her about it, and it was bad for a while. I was on the road to breaking my child.

She was and is one of the strongest people I know, but parents have such power, I could have done it. I could have broken her." Another murmur passed through the gathered listeners, and when Kimberly went on, her voice was rough with emotion. "But then one day I heard my sweet child, only four years old, praying to go home to Jesus rather than have to live one more day as a boy in this world, and that was the beginning of a new path for me. That was how I came to accept my girl for the miracle she is, and set my foot on the road to being her fierce mama bear protector.

"And here's the thing, y'all. If I could change my mind, so can anyone else. I was just as deep into that megachurch way of thinking as it is possible to go, and I saw the light. So, senators, and anyone watching this, please, just use your eyes and ears. Look at my child, listen to my child. She is a girl through and through, and perfect in the eyes of the Lord, exactly as she is. And if you pass this law, it could be a death sentence for kids like her. Remember, she was willing to go home to heaven before giving up her right to be her true self in the world."

thirty

LISTENING TO KIMBERLY'S speech, Joy and her mother had taken each other's hands, and when Kimberly was done and people were clapping, they looked at each other, and Joy saw that her mother's cheeks were wet. She felt close to tears herself. "I love you exactly as you are," Mom said. "Just so you know."

Joy swallowed. "Thanks, Mom. I love you too."

There were two more speakers after Kimberly, but Joy didn't hear what they said, because it was almost time for the Sparkle Squad to cheer, and she had to get them ready. She and Max were the leaders. It was their job.

She went to where the squad was grouped together, watching the next person talk, and gestured with her hand to get them to move farther away. Max caught her eye and nodded—she understood what Joy was doing and joined in nudging the team off to a little distance.

When they were almost out of sight around a corner of the building, they gathered in a small circle, and Joy said in a quiet but urgent voice, "Sparkle Squad, it's almost time for our big moment. Are you ready?"

Everyone looked at everyone else and nodded. Max spoke in a voice like Joy's, almost a whisper but full of energy. "We can do better than that," she said. "Are. You. Ready?" This time everyone pumped their fists or made fierce faces or did little dance moves, and whispered. "Ready!"

Joy said, "I just want to say, I am honored that you all came all the way to Austin today to help me fight for my rights against this awful bill. When I was kicked off the team, I was so mad that I thought I wanted to give up cheer, but now with you all I have realized that I had something more to learn. This is real cheerleading, right here. It's not about a football game or a basketball game. Those things still matter, but this matters more. This is cheering for our lives."

The squad's reactions were quieter this time, more thoughtful, but everyone's eyes were shining with intensity now. Max put her hand in, and everyone else followed suit. Max and Joy exchanged another glance and a nod. In unison they said, "Sparkle Squad on three—one, two, three!"

"Sparkle Squad!" all five of them whisper-shouted, flinging their hands up, out, and away and doing the wiggling fingers Max had invented.

"Let's go," Joy said. The last speaker had just finished, and Uncle Mac was looking their way and beckoning. "Time to do this."

The other people there for the rally had cleared a little space. The Sparkle Squad lined up with Joy in the middle and Max at her right hand. They checked their positions and made sure the line was straight. The man with the TV camera turned the dark eye of its lens on them, and many other people had their phones out, recording. Joy ignored them. Now that the moment had come, she felt focused and calm. She glanced one more time right and left, and saw that everyone was ready, waiting for her signal. "Five, six, seven, eight," she chanted, and they went into the cheer, with words and choreography by everyone together in the squad. Each of them had added something.

> *Rainbow kids deserve to live*
> *Rainbow kids have so much to give.*
> *Doesn't matter, girl or boy*
> *Rainbow kids should share the joy.*
> *Even if you're in between,*
> *Cheer with me if you know what I mean.*
> *Rainbow kids will always be*
> *Strong and brave and whole and free.*
> *So don't try to change us*
> *Don't try to explain us*
> *Just let us be our fabulous selves.*
> *Go, go, go, rainbow kids!*

The routine ended with Joy sitting on Max's and Norah's shoulders. The TV man had stepped closer and was pointing the camera right at Joy. She ignored it, concentrating on smiling out at the crowd, who were applauding and cheering. With each beat of her heart, a flash of warm pleasure pulsed through her whole body. The last twenty seconds had been the most fun she could ever remember having in her whole life.

After hugs and high fives and congratulations all around, Joy saw that the rally was ending. People were tucking signs under their arms and walking away. They had shown up and delivered their message. Of course, it was impossible to know if they had changed any senators' minds, but it still felt good to have tried. And nothing bad had happened. No one had shown up to shout at them. Mission accomplished.

In the car on the way home, Joy soaked up the love and praise that everyone had for her, but she was careful to say, "It wasn't just me. It was the whole team," and she meant it. Cheer was about belonging, and it was about teamwork. She could feel that all the way down into her bones.

To top it all off, just as they were entering the outskirts of Houston, about half an hour from home, Uncle Mac's phone chimed, and he checked it and said, "The committee killed the bill. We did it. No one is going to pass a law this session to take trans kids away from their parents."

Everyone in the car cheered so loud that Joy covered her ears, even though she was adding to the noise herself. When the hubbub had died down, Will said, "What do you mean, 'this session'?"

"Oh, they can always try again."

Joy's mood dimmed a little. "They can?"

Uncle Mac twisted in his seat to look back at her. His face was calm. "Yes, they can. It's just how it goes. We have to fight the same fights over and over again, every two years. But that doesn't take anything away from our victory today. We won this round, and that's more than enough reason to celebrate."

thirty-one

BACK IN APPLETON, Aunt Caroline was waiting to join Joy, her mom, and Uncle Mac for the drive to the school board meeting. She was happy to hear about how well the rally had gone, and Joy savored her praise, but then a silence fell. Mom, driving, looked worried. After a minute she said, "I have to confess, I'm feeling anxious about this meeting tonight. I checked the parents' forum again this afternoon, and I'm afraid there are going to be some worked-up people there, people with very wrong ideas about trans kids. There have been some alarming posts."

In a steady voice, Aunt Caroline asked, "Were there any direct threats?"

Mom shook her head. "No, just a bunch of . . .

I guess I would call it rabble-rousing. People are saying that trans kids are a threat to everyone else. They're talking about saving their children from us."

Aunt Caroline and Uncle Mac were both nodding. Uncle Mac said, "Yeah, that's pretty typical. But we'll keep you safe, don't worry."

Mom glanced at Joy in the rearview mirror. "Sweetheart, there's one more thing you should know."

Joy swallowed, braced herself, and said, "What?"

Mom said, "There are two people who I would say are the leaders of the rabble-rousers, and I'm afraid one of them is Steph's mom."

Joy sighed with relief. "Oh, is that all?" she said. "That's okay. Steph and I are not friends anymore. Every time I see her at school, her face gets all hard and she turns away."

Aunt Caroline said, "I'm sorry you lost a friend, but unfortunately, that can happen."

Joy said, "Well, I guess she wasn't that good a friend, huh? If she couldn't stand to be with me anymore once she learned that I'm trans."

When they got to the school, the parking lot

was almost full. As they made their way toward the entrance, they saw a group of people standing with signs. Joy peered ahead to see what the signs said, then took her mom's hand. Steph and her mother were there. Steph's mother had a tight, hard face and angry eyes. Steph was looking down at her feet. Joy paused a second and said, "Steph." Her former friend didn't look up. "Can't you even look at me?"

Steph's mother pointed a finger and growled through clenched teeth, "You stay away from my child, you monster." Mom gripped Joy's hand tighter and hurried forward.

In the auditorium, many seats were already taken. Joy looked up at her mother's face, which looked worried, even scared. Aunt Caroline said, "How about over here?" She pointed to a section in back, where a couple of people were holding rainbow flags.

As they sat down, Joy saw a man she didn't know holding a sign. It said, *I stand with Joy Simmons.* When the man saw her, he looked startled for a second, then smiled and nodded. Joy nodded back. Just like at the committee hearing, it was good to know there were friends in the room.

The man turned and spoke to someone next to him, who looked at Joy and smiled too, and then a sort of ripple passed through the room as the realization spread that they were there. People sitting in the seats ahead of them turned around to look, which made Joy feel self-conscious and uncomfortable. She leaned to hide a little behind Aunt Caroline, who was sitting next to her. "Steady," Uncle Mac said quietly.

Mom said, "I forgot to sign up to speak."

Uncle Mac said, "I'll do it for you," and slipped away. He was back in a minute. "The list is pretty long, I'm afraid," he said. "You're eighth." Mom shook her head unhappily.

Just like last time, everyone who had gathered was going to have to wait until the end of the meeting. The people in the room sat quietly, many of them playing on their phones, while the school board discussed school board business. Joy was one of the phone players part of the time. The rest of the time she spent studying the face of Superintendent Fellows. It was just as heavy and still and hard as the first time she had seen it, a month ago.

When the time finally came for public comments, a stir passed through the room. This was what almost everyone had come for. The woman with the clipboard called the first name on the list. The first speaker was a mother of one of Joy's classmates. She seemed awkward and shy at the microphone. "I don't want to judge other people's lifestyle choices," she said, "but I do think we ought to have safety procedures in place before we let these people do whatever they want."

Uncle Mac muttered under his breath. Other people in the room were reacting the same way. The room was starting to feel tense.

The second speaker was young, with pink hair and tattoos on her arms. "My name is Elsie, and I'm a concerned citizen," she said, talking fast and loud. "And I'm here to speak out tonight against the shameful way that the Appleton School District is targeting trans kids."

Joy perked up, recognizing an ally, but the superintendent was scowling. Elsie used the word "transphobic" and he picked up his gavel. Elsie used the word "fascist," and the superintendent banged the table. "I will not have this body spoken to in this manner," he growled. A few angry voices in the crowd agreed with him.

"I have a right to be heard!" Elsie shouted. A

different group of voices in the audience called out words of agreement.

The superintendent ignored her. "Next!" he barked at the woman with the clipboard, who hastily called out the name of Steph's mother.

Steph's mother came to the podium and started making an angry speech, and quite quickly the crowd started reacting strongly. Those who clearly agreed with her clapped and shouted encouragements to the points she was making. Those who had come to support Joy and trans kids like her started booing and jeering.

The speech . . . well, the speech was a mix of alarming, made-up facts and anger. The main point seemed to be that Joy and kids like her were a terrible threat. She kept talking about predators, and Joy, feeling horrified, thought, *Does she mean me?*

The superintendent had been quick with the gavel before, but this time he just let Steph's mom speak, and the room got rowdier. A few people in the audience started turning to look at Joy. Fingers were pointed. Hurtful words were shouted.

Joy looked up at her mom and said, "I don't like this."

Mom nodded. "Me neither," she said. She looked at Uncle Mac. "We need to go," she said. "Please get us out of here."

Uncle Mac nodded, stood up, and led the four of them toward the exit. The noise behind them grew to a peak. True, some of them were shouting good things. "We love you, Joy!" someone shouted. "The bigots will never win!" shouted another. But the other hateful voices were still there too, and Joy needed to get away. Words on a screen were one thing. Angry grown-up strangers shouting and scowling in person was something else entirely.

Hey Jojo,

The best part of the Big Day (next to finally meeting Kai in person!) was when the Sparkle Squad cheered at the Capitol, and we found out on the way home that the committee killed the bill, so there will be no law in Texas that says they can take me away from Mom because she takes care of me. At least, not right away. Uncle Mac says we might have to fight against the same bill again, and that seems wrong to me. Haven't we helped them see that it's just a terrible, horrible idea? But I guess if we have to fight again, we'll fight again. And meanwhile, it felt so good to lead the cheer today. I loved, loved, loved doing that.

The worst part was the school board meeting. All these people with mean faces showed up, and Steph's mom made this icky mean speech and people started shouting things, so we had to leave. I don't understand how a grown-up woman could believe the things she was saying about me, and I don't understand how she could get so angry. She

seemed like a nice normal woman when I was
going over to Steph's house back in the summer. She made snacks for us and smiled. But
now she thinks I'm a monster. That was the
word she used.

The other thing about the meeting was,
Mom didn't even get to speak, so it doesn't
look like I'll get to get back on the cheer team
or use the right bathroom anytime soon. I
wonder if I could change schools. I'm just so
tired of being treated this way.

God bless Mom and Will, and Uncle Mac
and Aunt Caroline, and the Sparkle Squad,
and the senators who voted to kill the bill, and
everyone who showed up at the meeting to be
on our side.

thirty-two

THE NEXT MORNING at school, something weird was going on. As Joy walked in the front entrance, a kid she didn't even know gave her a big smile and a fist pump and said, "Yes! Way to go, Joy!" Before she had gone many steps, another kid did something almost the same. "All right!" he said. A couple of passing girls smiled, and one of them gave her a thumbs-up. Then, down the hall, Joy made eye contact with Whitney, but the other girl's superior attitude and permanent mean look were gone. Whitney made a face and turned away. What in heaven's name was happening?

Rounding a corner, Joy came face-to-face with Emily Porter, the cheer team coach. They were both moving so fast they almost ran into each other. "Coach Porter," Joy stammered. "Sorry."

"No worries," Coach Porter said. "It's good to see you, Joy. And I'm glad we ran into each other, because I wanted to say, I saw your cheer at the Capitol, and I thought it was really good."

"Thank you. You were at the Capitol?"

"No, I wasn't," Coach Porter answered. "I saw it online. You've gone viral. Didn't you know?"

Joy remembered the round black eye of the TV camera. "No, I didn't know."

"Well, you have. And, it was a great cheer. Did you make it all up yourself?"

"It was a team effort," Joy said. "Max and me, we started a Sparkle Squad after I got kicked off the team."

Coach Porter was nodding. "Yeah, I've heard a little about that. Congratulations. I think it's great that you took the initiative and that you've kept on cheering."

"Wow," Joy said. "Thanks, Coach Porter."

"Coach Emily is fine. And I just want you to know, I have never agreed with the decision to take you off the team. But I have to follow the school's guidelines." Coach Emily smiled. "Joy, I think you have a talent for cheer, and a bright future ahead of you, if you stick with it and work hard."

"Oh, I will," Joy said breathlessly. "Thank you. You better believe I will."

As the morning continued, Joy marveled at the sensation of suddenly being a celebrity at school. The usual hostile faces were still there around the edges, looking a little more hostile than usual, but mostly it was people she hardly knew, excited to see her and eager to share their excitement.

And, of course, as soon as she could, she searched on her phone and found the video of the cheer. She could hardly believe her eyes. The video had been picked up by a national site. It had over forty thousand views, and the number was ticking up steadily.

"Oh my God!" Joy shouted. For a minute she savored the hot feeling of victory pulsing through her entire being. Then she watched the video five times in a row without stopping. It was thrilling to see how it had gone, even if she noticed that the squad was not quite in sync for the second half, and that she had made one mistake that she hadn't been aware of at the time, leaving out a move that everyone else remembered to do.

As the morning went on, many more students

and a few of the school's adults shared their excitement about the Sparkle Squad's viral achievement. There were also a handful of if-looks-could-kill looks, from Whitney again and Steph and some others, and a couple of shouted insults, but Joy just ignored them.

At lunch, as Joy approached the usual group in the far field, she could see that it had gotten larger. Several new kids who had never joined them before were there. The whole group was eagerly waiting for her and broke into spontaneous cheers and applause as she arrived. She clapped too and called out, "Go, Sparkle Squad!" Then everyone was watching the viral video again on multiple devices—now up to over sixty thousand views.

At dinner that evening—by which time the video had over a hundred thousand views—Mom listened to Joy's account of the day and told her again how proud she was. Then she said, "I have some good news, too, actually."

"You do?"

"Yes. Two things."

"Tell, tell!"

"Well, number one, I got a phone call today from

the head of a cheer gym in Houston, and she said that she had seen the video and was interested in having you join their gym."

Joy gaped at her mother. It was the best news ever . . . except for one thing. "That's amazing!" Joy said. "But what about . . ."

"The money?" Mom said. "Yes, of course I thought of that right away, and the woman seemed so nice, so I just said it. I said, 'That's very kind of you, but I'm afraid we couldn't afford it.'"

"And?"

"And she said, 'I thought that might be the case, but we do have ways we might be able to help.' So we have an appointment to go talk to her, and I think they might be able to make it so you can join."

Joy shrieked, bolted up out of her chair, and ran around the table to throw her arms around her mother's neck. "Thank you, thank you, thank you!" she said, practically in tears. Mom and Will laughed, and Mom said, "Don't thank me. It's because of you, because of what you did with the Sparkle Squad. You earned it."

It took Joy a minute to calm down and remember that there was another piece of news. As she prepared to tell it, Mom had an unusual light in her eyes, like, this one is even better. "The other news is, I got an email from Kimberly Shappley, and we're invited to come hang out at their house in Austin on Saturday."

Now Joy was so happy she couldn't figure out how to show it. She sat back down in her chair with her mouth open. Then she leapt up and bounded around the dining room, whooping, while her family watched her with loving eyes.

Hey Jojo,

What an amazing day! The Sparkle Squad got even bigger, and everyone was so happy about what we did, not just the five of us who went, but everyone. And then Mom came home and said maybe I could cheer at a gym where they will accept me for who I am, and I was so happy, and then she said we're going to hang out at Kai's house on Saturday, and I was even happier!

Also, after dinner, Will suggested we make another video. He said, "We made one video where you talked to the superintendent, and then we made another video where you talked to the senators. What if we made a third video where you talk to the whole world?" Mom liked that. She said, "Interesting. Joy, if you could say anything you want to all the people on the planet, what would it be?"

That's a big question, but I'm thinking about it. I want to do it. I want to say something to the whole world, once I figure out what.

God bless . . . you know what? God bless everyone. Even the haters. It must be so hard, being a person who hates. That must really be some kind of icky life. So, God bless everyone, including them, and I hope they can find a way to hate less and love more someday.

thirty-three

ON SATURDAY MORNING, Joy was so eager for the Austin visit that she was ready to go an hour before her mother, and then pestered her so much that her mother finally said a rare sharp word. She said she was sorry right after, and that she knew Joy was excited, but she also reminded her that they had arranged to arrive at a certain time, and that it was rude to show up early. Joy did her best to contain herself. It was not easy.

Mom had plugged the Shappleys' address into her phone at the start of their drive. When they'd gotten within minutes of Kai's house, Mom drove through a maze of curvy roads while Joy gazed out the window, taking in the neighborhood. She saw lots of kitschy, quirky houses, much like the one that belonged to the Shappleys. They lived in a tiny house that they had named the MiniPearl, after a famous country-and-western singer from long ago. For the most part, all the houses had front porches and gardens. Here and there, stately old trees provided some shade over well-loved picnic tables.

The MiniPearl, when they reached it, turned out to be painted dark brown and to have a slanty roof, higher on the right than the left, with a porch made of pressure-treated lumber built all around it. As they pulled up, Kai and another kid, who Joy guessed had to be Kai's brother, Kaleb, appeared, waving madly. Mom parked and Joy jumped out. Kimberly joined her children on the porch, smiling a welcome. Kai and Joy met on the grass in front of the porch steps and hugged each other fiercely.

Kai was eager to give Joy a tour of the house, so they went inside. The house was very small but ingeniously put together. Joy's favorite part was the loft where Kai and Kaleb slept, up in the right-hand peak of the roof. It felt like a secret clubhouse. There was a friendly dog to meet, and a couple of shy cats to glimpse before they disappeared into hiding somewhere. Joy loved it all.

Kimberly had made a lunch that included fresh

hard-boiled eggs from their chickens. It was a fine warm day, so they sat at a table in the MiniPearl's backyard. By this point the moms were deep in conversation. Kimberly was telling mom that she was so concerned about more bad laws being passed that she was seriously thinking of moving to another state. Mom shook her head sadly and gave Joy a worried look. At the same moment, Kai ate the last bite of her sandwich and said to Joy, "Come on, I want to show you my chickens."

"I would love that," Joy said. "And then . . ."

"Then what?"

Joy felt suddenly bashful. She had had the idea she wanted to say in the car, and it seemed to her like a generous idea, a gift, but she wasn't sure. She was worried that it might come across wrong, like bragging or something. She looked at Kai, who was smiling expectantly, and thought, *We're already friends, and I really think we could get to be like sisters, so I have to say it.* "And then, if you like, I could teach you some cheer moves."

Kai's face lit up. "I would love that!" she said. "Chickens first, though. And I can show you my sewing machine too."

"You have a sewing machine?"

"Yeah, Mom just got it for me."

"I'm so jealous! I've wanted a sewing machine my whole life."

"Well, let's go play with it then."

The two girls slipped away from the serious adult conversation still going on at the lunch table, going off to share what they loved with each other and to just be kids together for a while, whatever awful stories people far away, people who didn't know them at all, might be making up about them.

Hey Jojo,

Kai Shappley is totally amazing, and I love her. At the end of our visit today, we swore to be friends until the end of our lives. I can't wait to see what kind of grown-up woman she will be. I said that to Mom in the car on the way home, and she said, "I can't wait to see what kind of grown-up woman you will be either."

We found out yesterday that for sure I won't be back on the Appleton cheer team, and it looks like I'm stuck with the nurse's bathroom too, all because of one old man full of hate. I would say I hate him back, but I've been thinking about that, and I decided I don't want to hate anyone. What I can say is that I'm still sad about not being on the school team anymore, but not as sad as I was. I still love cheer, but I love activism now too, and our Capitol cheer video has almost half a million views, so I know I'm making a difference. In activism there's also the same feeling of being on a team and fighting for something we all believe in, and that feels so right to me.

And anyway, I still get to cheer too. The

other thing that happened yesterday was that we visited the gym that got in touch with Mom, and they said I could cheer with them for free. My first practice is on Monday. The only thing that would make that better would be if Max could do it with me, and she's going to ask her mom, so, fingers crossed.

I'm so lucky. I have my family who love me, not just Mom and Will, but Aunt Caroline and Uncle Mac and Kai and Max and the new Sparkle Squad and everyone else. Family of choice, Aunt Caroline called that, and as long as I have it, I can have faith that love will win in the end.

God bless everyone, no exceptions. But please, God, give an extra-special blessing to the trans kids. When total strangers hate you for made-up reasons, you need all the help you can get.

HELLO, WORLD. *I am making this video because with so many lies being told about people like me, I need to tell you my truth.*

My name is Joy Simmons. I am twelve years old, and I am a transgender girl. I live in Appleton, Texas, with my mom and my brother, Will, and I love my family, my dog, doing art and needlework, and especially cheer and being an activist.

Recently I have learned that there are people who, it seems like, can't figure out how to fit me into how they understand the world, and so I guess they feel like they have to say things about me that just aren't true—horrible mean things. People say I'm a freak, or a monster, or even a predator. I asked Mom to explain it to me, and she said I was too young, that she would tell me when I'm older. How can I be a thing, if I'm too young to even know what it is? I'm just a kid!

So I've been thinking about it, and what I want to say is this: We live in America, the land of the free. I've learned about freedom in school. I've learned about freedom of speech, and freedom of religion. But there's one other freedom that I think is just as important, and that's the freedom to say and be who we are.

World, when you make up stories about me, it's like you are saying you know who I am better than I do. First of all, you don't. No one knows me better than I do. And the second thing is, when you do that, you take away my freedom to say who I am and to be that person. Please, stop making up horrible stories about me. It's mean, and it's unfair, and it hurts me and other kids like me. It makes our lives dangerous and hard, when we should just be concentrating on being kids.

World, if things were right, no one would try to tell me that I'm not me. If I was really a true free American, that would include me being free to tell you who I am, and then have you believe me and accept me. And I'm telling you, I have been telling you every day since I could talk, that I am a girl. In all the ways that count, I am a girl. Can't you see that? Just look at me! Listen to me! Believe your eyes and ears, not the horrible stories people make up about me because they are uncomfortable or afraid, or because they want to use me to scare you. Please, see me, hear me. I'm right here, being who I am. I can't show you or tell you any plainer. I am a girl. I am a girl. I am a girl.

God bless you, world, and could you please just let me live my life? Please, and thank you, from the bottom of my heart.

Oh, and, one more thing: Go, Sparkle Squad!

Kai Shappley's Advice for Being an Activist

Be yourself.

Tell your story.

Fight for others.

Kai Shappley's Favorite Dolly Parton Songs

1. "Coat of Many Colors"
2. "Jolene"
3. "Love Is Like a Butterfly"
4. "Mary, Did You Know?"
5. "9 to 5"

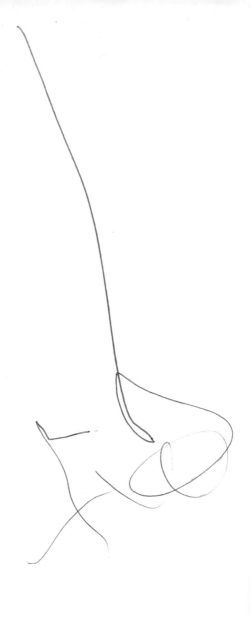

31901069328443